HIGHWAY SPEED

Also by Stephen Roger Powers

POETRY

The Follower's Tale
(Salmon Poetry, 2009)

Hello, Stephen
(Salmon Poetry, 2014)

All Seats Fifty Cents
(Salmon Poetry, 2019)

HIGHWAY SPEED

Stories

STEPHEN ROGER POWERS

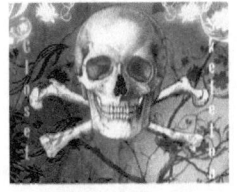

Closet Skeleton Press
Atlanta

First Edition
ISBN 978-0-578-58398-3

Library of Congress Control Number: 2019915035

Published in 2019 by
Closet Skeleton Press
Atlanta

www.closetskeleton.com

Front and back cover art and design by Mike Driscoll
atomicleprechaun@gmail.com

For my parents,
who took me for my first rides,

my brother,
who loves the road like I do,

and Cornelius, Beverly, Paul, Alice, John, and Steve,
who take me on the road again and again.

Acknowledgements

I thank Mary Beth first. For getting me off to a good start writing fiction, I thank Thomas Bontly, Ron Rindo, and Sheila Roberts. Thanks are due also to Natasha Chisdes, Anna Cogdill, Robert Perry Ivey, Zeke Jarvis, Paula Sergi, and Matthew Silverman for taking a look at early drafts of these stories and offering suggestions. For sharing ideas, I thank Chrissy Burns, Eleanor Cummins, Marilyn De La Mair, Amy Hill, Margie Littell, Colten Vanosdale, Ed Whitelock, Jessica Wilson, and Bruce Woodford. I am grateful to Craig Amason and Mark Jurgensen for answering my questions about Andalusia. Much gratitude as well to Jessie Lendennie and the Salmon Bookshop & Literary Centre, where I worked on major revisions to this book. Finally, I thank Mike Driscoll for making this book look good and Closet Skeleton Press for putting it out there.

Credit is due to the editors of the following, in which some of these stories or earlier versions of them first appeared:

Bryant Literary Review: "One More Time for Donny Deadborne"

Eureka Literary Magazine: "Snake Wine"

The Licking River Review: "Rhinestone Horses"

Main Street Rag: "Little Earthquakes"

Marginalia: "Sister Melvina"

Southern Gothic: "The Tennessee Scrambler"

"...worst accident I ever seen."

SPÉED
LIMIT
55

LITTLE EARTHQUAKES

O N FRIDAY OF THE MOST eventful week of their lives together, the parachutist plummeted from the sky and landed in the wooded cemetery across the street from their house.

His unfortunate and surprising death literally right in their front yard didn't change anything, however.

Georgiana still woke up in the morning with her arm around her pillow, thinking it was Grant and mumbling to it softly, and Trinket said that this was sorrowful because it meant Georgiana hadn't moved on *at all* and that Trinket had done nothing but waste her time. Besides, they'd just seen a parachutist die, for Christ's sake.

And on the Monday of that week, late in the afternoon, four days before the parachutist came screaming from the spring clouds, their neighbor Mr. Bauer started slowly digging for gold under the cottonwood by his mailbox. That was the day Georgiana finally told Trinket that she'd had dinner a few times with Grant at the Croissant de Lune, that she thought it all had gone fine so far, and that she was seriously thinking about getting back together with him and taking it very slow. A fresh start.

On Tuesday, the ground started humming every hour on the hour for about four minutes. Georgiana wondered if Mr. Bauer digging for gold had anything to do with it. Trinket confessed she was furious about Georgiana seeing Grant again.

By Wednesday morning, the hole was five feet deep, mounds of dirt in a circle around the edge. Mr. Bauer stood in the hole, shovel scooping, clumps of dirt flying, T-shirt soaked through, only his shoulders and bald head visible above the hole. Georgiana thought it was a wonder he hadn't hit any roots.

That was when Georgiana and Trinket also started setting up tables in the garage and marking potholders, chipped ashtrays, dusty videos, warped polka records, tangled necklaces, and faded blouses with price stickers. They'd been planning this rummage sale for a while. Georgiana got out her wedding dress, the one she would have worn down the aisle when she married Grant, and inspected it carefully before putting it back in its plastic bag, zipping it up, and writing Best Offer on the price sticker. Selling it didn't feel right but neither did keeping it, not with things so up in the air.

On Thursday, the ground was still humming every hour on the hour for about four minutes. It wasn't a loud hum, just enough to make you feel vibrations under your feet and shake the windows. But it was annoying. Mr. Bauer denied having anything to do with it and resumed his digging after carting all the dirt away to his back garden with a wheelbarrow and carrying a ladder from his garage so he could climb in and out of the hole easier.

And Georgiana decided she'd really known all along that she was going to start seeing Grant again at some point in the near future, on a trial basis, as she'd put it to him at the Croissant de Lune, to see if things could be worked on. It was just that she didn't know how to tell Trinket, who had been good to her. She only knew she was still in love with his wavy and sandy hair streaked with a little gray, his quick white smile, and his dazzling blue eyes that reminded her of marbles when he laughed.

Georgiana Starling. You might say she was a little troubled. Secretive. Maybe manipulative. Trinket probably would say this most of all, especially now. Georgiana was attractive in a cosmopolitan and sophisticated sort of way, but also a tad tomboyish. Tall and thin. One crooked tooth in her smile. Sharp features and a pointed nose. Shoulder-length auburn hair with some brown roots showing.

Her father had never been around. He'd only come by once a year, at most, and she knew this was only obligatory so he'd feel less guilty about his absence. One time when she was five, she was being difficult, and her father didn't want to deal with it, so he locked her in her closet and frightened her by putting on a scary mask, opening the door in the dark, and yelling boo and shrieking and hooting wildly. Her therapist told her this fueled her need for approval and her fear of making people angry. And it explained why she was afraid of the dark.

On Friday morning then, just as Georgiana and Trinket were opening up their rummage sale, two policemen drove out with a city engineer. They told Mr. Bauer he had to stop digging until he reinforced his hole, now ten feet deep and ten feet across, and obtained the necessary permits. Mr. Bauer climbed out in a huff and accused Trinket of calling to complain. The city engineer, a puffy and nervous man, said he had no explanation for the ground humming when Georgiana asked about it. As soon as the policemen and the city engineer left, Mr. Bauer went right back at it again after he took a swig from his Michelob bottle. He insisted there was gold on his property, and he was going to find it.

Trinket McKahen. She was willowy and good-looking like Georgiana, but with a slightly sharper bad-girl edge. Trinket and Georgiana looked similar, except Trinket wore a rough leather jacket, roared around town on her Harley, kept her long chestnut hair in a ponytail, and could drink any man into the floor. She had a habit of leaving pennies everywhere. They fell out of her pockets where she'd been sitting. They collected in the corners of the house. One was even in the bathtub, sitting on the hair trap, gleaming like a spiffy little manhole cover.

"Why in the name of God," Trinket said to Georgiana on Tuesday while they were doing dishes together, "were you even staying in contact with a man who called you dumb, who told you to lose some weight, and fought with your mother, threw things at you, couldn't last more than a minute, wanted you to get your breasts enlarged, not to mention made you drink stupid Japanese sex herbs in your tea, and couldn't find a clitoris if an off-ramp took him right to it?"

The pennies were what had initially attracted Georgiana

to Trinket. Two months after she broke it off with Grant, she found herself lost and drunk and craving excitement. A different kind of excitement. She noticed Trinket in Axle's Bar. Trinket was slamming shots of tequila until the heavy biker she was with fell off his stool. Trinket only laughed and ordered one more, slammed that down too, and went to the women's room, mysteriously leaving a trail of pennies, somehow, behind her on the floor. Georgiana followed without knowing why, led by the pennies, only feeling a sense of overwhelming and wet curiosity she'd never felt before, and once she got in the women's room Trinket just kissed her out of the blue, lips snapping with tequila and cigarette smoke.

And Georgiana felt the apparent answer to Trinket's question rising up her throat while she wiped a plate dry, but she pushed it back down. It was there, but she didn't let it come out.

I don't know, I don't know, I don't know, I just do.

So here we are, back to Friday. Rummage sale, gold digging, policemen and the city engineer, the parachutist.

"You've never said one nice thing about Grant," Trinket said for the tenth time that week while they were sitting on metal folding chairs by a card table in their driveway. The cash box was shiny. The spring morning was chilly and overcast. The ground was still dark and soggy. Any minute now it would start shaking again. "Why would *he* want to keep seeing someone who's said only bad things about him behind his back?" Trinket added.

Georgiana didn't answer. She was tired of it.

A small red BMW with the top down rolled up the street,

turned around, and parked under Mr. Bauer's cottonwood. The woman behind the wheel was wearing a motorcycle helmet the same color as the car. Georgiana thought that was odd. The woman took off the helmet and climbed out. She came slowly up the driveway, dressed for the chilly morning in a scarf, a flannel shirt, and a fishing vest with a fleece patch above the chest pocket. Trinket asked her why she drove with a helmet on.

"Case I flip the car," she said.

She poked around the spatulas and muffin pans, shuffled the faded jackets of the polka records, and examined the tag of a pink blouse. Then she left. She spent a few minutes chatting with Mr. Bauer, who was out of sight down in his hole, before she got in the BMW, adjusted the helmet's chin strap, and drove away.

Some clouds parted, and the sun came through. It warmed up a bit. The ground shook. The spring robins stopped what they were doing. After about four minutes, the ground stopped shaking, and the robins went about their business again. Mr. Bauer came over and said he was sure some military exercises were responsible for the ground shaking. That or aliens, he said.

Trinket and Georgiana's only other customer all day was a thin young man with a goatee who asked if he could use the bathroom to try on the wedding dress. He said he'd read in their classified ad that they had one for sale. Trinket showed him where the bathroom was, but he came back out wearing just his boxers and the bodice and asked for assistance.

Georgiana went in with him and helped him hook the

bodice shut in back. She pulled the dress with its train up his skinny, hairless legs, and she hooked it to the bodice at the waist and smoothed it all down. She placed the tiara on his head and brought the veil down over his face.

He looked at himself in the mirror. He put his hand under the veil and rubbed his goatee. "I'll have to shave," he said. But the dress fit him perfectly.

Georgiana didn't know what to think. She'd only tried on her dress once, in the store, and she called off the engagement the day after bringing it home. Grant had lost his temper about something, she couldn't remember what anymore, and had thrown one of his softballs at her so hard and fast she didn't see it coming, and it smacked her on the side of her neck under her jaw. She locked herself in the bathroom and cried by herself for an hour while he swore and yelled and knocked things over and, finally, went out somewhere. This was when she realized his behavior was starting to appear typical. Later, he walked back in and acted as if nothing had happened, also typical, and ignored the ugly bruise and the swelling on her neck, came up from behind her, pulled her hair back, and kissed her on the cheek. When he was at work the next day, she moved her things into her mother's house.

And now someone else was trying on her wedding dress, and she was about to let it go.

"Will you take a hundred bucks for it?" the man said.

Georgiana sighed and thought. "Two hundred and fifty," she said.

She helped the man take it off ("Bet you never helped a bride take his dress off before," he joked), and she hauled it swishing and crinkling into the kitchen and packed it back up in the bag for him while he shut the bathroom door and put his clothes back on.

He left with the dress. Georgiana hid the two hundred and fifty dollars under the tray in the cash box. She felt as if her load had been lightened but at the expense of something else she couldn't quite put her finger on. Maybe she should have asked for more money, she thought. But, no, she reminded herself, letting it go quickly was the best way to start anew. Even if it was with the same guy.

"That was weird," Trinket said. A penny fell out of the pocket of her black jeans while she was sitting with one leg crossed up on her other knee, and it bounced and rolled across the driveway into the barely-there grass.

And so the day passed. They sat at the card table. Georgiana made a run to McDonald's. Trinket said McDonald's food tasted best eaten outside in the middle of the afternoon on a card table in the driveway. Georgiana avoided saying anything to her. Mr. Bauer kept digging. He took an occasional beer break. The ground all over the neighborhood hummed every hour on the hour for about four minutes. Every time it happened, people came out of their houses up and down the block and looked around, then just went back inside.

Late in the afternoon, it was cloudy again. That's when the parachutist appeared out of nowhere up in the sky so fast and so quick Georgiana didn't know what it was at first, except that it yelled all the way to its death. It hit the tall Austrian pine in the cemetery across the street and ripped down through the branches like a bullet. The yelling ceased the moment the body hit the ground. She didn't see it hit because it landed under the tree, covered by the wide boughs around the base, but she heard it, a sickening *plump* sound.

Mr. Bauer flew out of his hole, Trinket jumped from her chair, and Georgiana ran after them. The pine's branches of were still rustling from the disturbance when the three of them came upon it. Mr. Bauer sprinted back to his house. Trinket stood with her hands over her mouth. Georgiana crawled under the tree, and there the person was, next to the trunk, bent in a way no body should be bent, one leg twisted under his chest, his arms splayed out and cut to shreds, his neck pulled and stretched too far. His chute had apparently never opened.

Needles continued sifting down from above, along with pieces of the branches the parachutist had broken. His goggles were cracked and pushed into his head, and blood darkened the damp carpet of dead brown needles under his face. He appeared about twenty-five years old, not that much younger than Georgiana and Trinket.

Georgiana touched him, rested her hand on his back. His spandex jumpsuit was cool, but she pressed her hand down and held it there until the warmth from his body came through.

She crawled out from under the tree. Trinket was leaning on a rose-colored granite gravestone, shaking her head fast and crying and muttering oh my god over and over. Georgiana brushed herself off and leaned on the gravestone next to her. She put her arm around her, pulled her close, let Trinket rest her head on her shoulder. They leaned there. The robins flew and hopped. The sun came out, went away, came out. Mr. Bauer ran over from his house, said the police and an ambulance were on their way. "He's dead, isn't he?" he also said, breathless and sweaty. He wondered aloud where the skydiver's plane would be landing.

Georgiana led Trinket home. They spent the rest of the afternoon quietly stunned, elbows on the card table, watching the police cars and the hearse and the three fire trucks and the ambulance and all the neighbors milling around. Georgiana thought about how she'd never seen a dead body so soon and fresh after death. She wondered what Trinket was thinking, if she'd ever seen a dead man like that.

That night, after the rummage sale tables were pushed back into the garage and the neighborhood was quiet again, Trinket fell asleep on the couch while watching a *Matlock* rerun. Georgiana covered her with an afghan, kissed the top of her head, and went to bed alone. She stirred when she felt Trinket finally come in at three.

But on Saturday morning, when Georgiana stepped out of the shower, Trinket was gone. Her note on the table said she was riding her Harley to Vegas to think and get away. Think about love. About starting over. About time. About early and sudden death. There were three worn and dull pennies also on the table by the note. The note asked Georgiana to please be moved out by the end of next week, the first of May.

While Georgiana was reading the note, both relieved and hurt that Trinket had left first, the ground started shaking quietly but hard enough to softly rattle the pictures on the walls. Georgiana got dressed during this, and, when it stopped about four minutes later, she opened up the garage for the rummage sale to start and pulled the laden tables by herself back out on the driveway. She swept the garage floor and threw away the crinkly brown leaf, the dirt, and two pennies in the dustpan.

She waited for the bargain hunters. She waited for something to fall from the sky. For more pennies to lead the way to somewhere. For the guilt pattern she suspected would only repeat. For boxes, packed and heavy. For moving again. For Grant, who she knew she probably wouldn't stay with for good this time. But Georgiana felt compelled to give it a shot anyway, just to see now that her year with Trinket had run its course. And she waited for the next little earthquake. For the hole Mr. Bauer was digging to collapse in on him.

Then, because it was still early and no one had arrived for the rummage sale, she took a walk across the street over to the cemetery and the Austrian pine. On the gravestone where she'd leaned with Trinket the day before, there was only one penny, brand new, shining in the sun.

SPEED
LIMIT
55

BOTTOM FEEDER

VERA WAS NOT SURPRISED WHEN, years ago, her sister Genesis had decided to follow their mother's example by taking things from her friends, like lipsticks, new leather coats, boyfriends.

That soon escalated into taking things from stores, like a pair of new high heels Genesis wore out the door, her old shoes in a box she'd put back on the shelf.

A pregnancy test.

A block of mild cheddar cheese.

Vera's sister Genesis eventually upgraded to out-and-out robbery of a gas station.

But their mother refused to believe it.

"She's innocent," their mother said whenever the subject came up, which wasn't often because almost everyone in the family, including their father, preferred to pretend someone in the family was not in prison.

Vera understood why they felt that way. She never wanted to accept that her older sister was in prison either. Genesis was on an extended leave of absence. Maybe off in some strange foreign country finding herself while sitting cross-legged in a linen robe and chanting with her eyes closed. Growing up.

But Vera always knew Genesis wasn't gone for good. And she always wondered what they would do at the time of her return.

The correct word for that was reentry.

One day, their mother called in tears when Vera was in college in Fond du Lac. "The state constitution," their mother said quickly over and over between sobs. "I found it right here. It's in the state constitution."

Vera had to ask her to slow down. She'd just fallen asleep after working an overnight shift, and she had chemistry lab in two hours. She talked their mother into taking a deep breath, to please, Mama, remember she needed sleep.

"Cruel and unusual punishment," their mother said.

"What about it?"

"It says there shall not be cruel and unusual punishment."

And Vera realized she was talking about the prison sentence. According to their mother, Genesis should never have been sentenced in the first place because she was *innocent*—and their mother's crying was not the crying of despair but the crying of hope.

Of self-deception too because their mother had the same habit of shoplifting. The only difference was their mother had never been caught. And she'd not yet robbed a gas station.

Their mother grew more and more angry that her attempts to get the conviction overturned went nowhere, and she took that out on Genesis by refusing to write or visit and by refusing to get in the car when the morning to pick her up finally arrived.

Vera had explained it to herself as just another series of their mother's eccentricities and contradictions. Vera dropped by anyway and offered their mother a last chance to change her mind.

A firm no. Their mother waved Vera away from her coffee and cinnamon toast.

Their father reclined in front of a daybreak show on television. A smiling woman was chopping onions and talking to the tall host in the suit about packing economical lunches. Their father didn't look up when Vera left their mother in the kitchen and passed through the shadowy living room and out the door to the dawn-gray driveway.

Almost six years to the day since the judge read the sentence and Genesis was taken out of the courtroom in handcuffs, Vera drove north a couple hours, checked in at the visiting center, flipped through a magazine until someone told her it was time to bring the car up, and, finally, was shocked at the slouching, rough-looking woman who was her sister.

Vera asked if Genesis might want to stop for a few minutes at the old lake where they used to fish with their father and swim with their mother. Old time's sake. Get her mind off things.

Cold November drizzle crackled on the roof and trickled down the hood. The windows fogged up.

Genesis looked like she was wilting into her seat. Her seatbelt hung unworn. She made no move to pull it across her and buckle it.

Her green irises were flat and lifeless, but her pupils were pointed. Her once shiny strawberry hair was thin and frizzy, with split ends and white streaks. It was short too — she used to keep it long down her back, Vera recalled.

A faded black T-shirt flattened on Genesis' chest and bagged around her stomach, and musty-smelling khaki pants filled the car with an odor that forced Vera to crack her window.

On Genesis' feet were scruffy black slippers and thick white socks that were turning gray.

Vera didn't know what to make of her. She wanted to ask Genesis what had happened to her in there.

Why hadn't she ever written or called?

Now that Genesis was a very different person who had nothing to say there in the front seat, Vera started the engine and put some miles behind them so Genesis could tell her everything, every second and every hour, of the six years they missed together.

Driving toward the lake was like turning back the clock. Genesis grew more youthful every mile that passed until she appeared the way Vera remembered her the day she was led out of the courtroom in handcuffs. Her hair shone again with full color. Her skin smoothed. Her pupils softened and her eyes warmed.

But no words came from Genesis. She crossed her arms over her stomach and stared at her slippers the whole ride.

Seventy miles to the southwest, Vera watched Genesis zip up the new hoodie she'd bought for her. Vera slammed the trunk shut and zipped up her own. The two sisters found a place to stand near the boat ramp.

Ripples rolled and splashed on the rocks. The light was dim and gray, but the air was surprisingly a good ten degrees warmer. The coal power plant loomed across the narrow lake. Fog wove itself between the two smokestacks and hung over the dull water like a sheer curtain held up to the sky by skeletal fingers.

Vera and Genesis stood with their hands shoved deep in their pockets and their hoods pulled over their heads. The fog blew softly over the water. Vera wanted to resume a long-ago conversation that had been interrupted and forgotten, but she couldn't decide which one.

Genesis lit a cigarette from a pack Vera had brought. The smoke rose into the fog and became one with it.

The fog thickened, concealed the lake surface, and blocked more late-afternoon light. When the wind blew, water patches appeared and were quickly covered by fog again. The power plant disappeared in the fog too sometimes and reemerged a few seconds later. The stacks and their blinking lights towered like birthday candles when they remained unobscured while the fog rolled past the plant.

Genesis inhaled and let out a smoke stream. She threw her cigarette butt.

Vera was surprised they'd been standing there long enough for Genesis to smoke an entire cigarette with no words spoken. Vera's attention had been wandering, though. Thoughts of monsters in the lake curled through her mind, but the thousand questions she'd written there during the long drive chased them away and now clotted in her skull on the way to her mouth.

She pushed against this clog, tried to open a gap for the first question—*Where do you think you want to live?*—visualized the gap widening—*What kind of place might you want?*—far enough for two or three questions—*In town? In the country? Maybe a place with big windows in every room?*—until the clog broke up and was washed away—*Should we start looking tomorrow?*—and the questions torrent followed:

"Gas or electric stove?"

No answer.

"Do you still have your old artwork somewhere to decorate with?"

Silence.

"Hardwood or carpet?"

Genesis lit another cigarette.

"Walk-in closets? Space to grow into as you get more clothes?"

This was not going the way Vera had expected. Irritated, Vera pulled her hood farther forward. She blocked her peripheral vision so that all she saw was a tunnel to the fog wall and power plant. But she knew Genesis was inhaling and exhaling. Sisters know things about each other, even things they can't see.

Already four, Vera's watch said. Three hours to go. Where was home for Genesis? Their parents' house? Her house?

An obvious detail—oh, shit—overlooked while planning reentry.

Mist drifted between them. It was getting darker. The sun, somewhere beyond the fog at their backs, was lowering. Genesis' face was deep inside her hood's shadow. Vera imagined she must look the same to Genesis.

"I found *Psycho* for you," Vera said. "We can watch it later." Genesis would need to acclimate to life outside, so she'd bought her sister's favorite movie in case she hadn't seen it since before her sentencing.

The ground around the lake was bare and soggy. The hot water that was piped out the plant and into the lake kept the area warm and created a perpetual fog veil even in sub-zero weather, which was forecast to come early this year. The lake was popular in the winter with fishermen who liked to float in their wetsuits on swim rings while casting their lures.

"Hitchcock," Vera said. "Tony Perkins. Norman Bates." Vera laughed awkwardly. "Remember how you used to say when Norman pushes Marion's car in the swamp we feel sympathy for him? We don't want his crime to be discovered because we feel just as guilty as he does?"

Vera waited.

Something splashed in the water about thirty feet from them and sent small waves rippling in circles.

Chilly jitters sleeted through Vera, and she almost picked up a stone to throw in the direction of the splash.

The lake and the plant were familiar. She'd been coming here since she was young, so the gloomy surroundings weren't stirring the tension she was feeling. As long as she wasn't in the water, she was fine. Genesis hadn't said a word, and that was unsettling. Vera didn't know what would spark her to say something. In the fading light, her hood pulled far past her face, wearing those old clothes, Genesis was a rough and grungy Ghost of Christmas Past.

The two red lights on the stacks blinked over and over through the heavy fog, which moved across the lights. The lights faded a bit. The stacks emerged again. They looked to Vera like giant magic wands.

"I never understood why you liked Norman Bates so much," Vera said.

Why not, she imagined Genesis answering, but Vera didn't want to argue.

She talked instead. If Genesis wanted to be a captive audience, then that was her choice. Prison had probably trained her well enough for that.

Vera pushed her hood down and pulled her hair free. She breathed deeply. The misty air tickled her throat, and the smell, like burning coal but also like damp dirt, rushed through her nose. She felt she could force the smell all the way down into her toes if she inhaled hard enough.

"Remember," Vera said, "when we brought the rowboat down here?"

It was the middle of January when they did that. Young Vera was amazed how the water stayed warm enough to play in that time of year while several inches of crusty snow covered the ground around.

Winter swimming in the warm water was glorious too. Cold afternoons. Snow falling all around the lake. Falling through fog. Tickling her bare shoulders.

"We spent a whole day and a whole evening out here in the water one time," Vera said.

She and Genesis swam with their mother as night seeped through the fog, swam all the way over to the buoy marking the restricted area close to the plant where fishing boats couldn't go. They clung to the buoy and rose up and down with it. Their mother explained that hot water from the plant was piped deep below into the restricted area. That's why people didn't swim past the buoy and dive down there—the water was too hot.

Vera remembered wanting a mask so she could swim underwater and see hot water and steam billowing out those pipes. She remembered imagining that the steam was cotton candy spinning onto paper wands. Maybe underwater the steam would feel like cotton candy too.

Genesis' hood was a tunnel mouth. Vera half expected a train to come whooping out.

After a minute, Vera said, "It sure was a long time ago."

The winter she turned eight, their father walked up the bank, his rubber fishing boots splishing on the wet rocks, his green jacket dripping, and his rod swinging over his shoulder.

Vera squealed when she saw the stringer of fish he carried, and she scampered down the bank to meet him. The stringer hung from his hand to the ground. When Vera reached him, she gasped, then froze, her eyes wide and her mouth hanging.

The stringer was not a whole bunch of fish—no—it was one hell of a big catfish, gray and wet, its mouth at their father's fingers and its tail dragging.

Vera stood still while their father ran her small hand with his big one up and down the fish's belly. She didn't really feel it. She only noticed that it was wet and didn't have any scales. She focused instead on the fish's eyes and mouth. The eyes were empty, and the mouth was turned up in what she thought was a sly gonna-getcha grin.

Their father laughed his hearty laugh and said how good

the fish would taste for supper, didn't Vera think so too? Such a big bottom feeder in a lake by a power plant. How yummy!

Genesis snickered and said how good Vera would taste for the fish's supper.

Vera shrieked, whipped her hand away, and scurried up the bank on her hands and feet. After that, Vera didn't like swimming in the lake or even just getting her toes wet, no matter how warm the water stayed or how much the rational side of her knew the creature on their father's stringer only seemed bigger than she was because she was small for an eight-year-old.

"I didn't come down for supper that night," Vera said. "I didn't want the fish to get me."

Once more, something splashed in the water not too far from them, and this time Vera bent over for a stone and tossed it in the direction of the noise. The stone made a bigger splash, and all was quiet.

The fog veil was still thick. The power plant lights still blinked.

Genesis lit a third cigarette.

"Somebody didn't want some aquarium piranhas anymore," Vera said, "so they dumped the piranhas here. Local legend says they grew and grew after that. When a boy went missing, word around town was the giant piranhas got him. But the news said the piranhas were all caught."

Vera continued talking. Maybe whoever released the piranhas hoped they'd eat somebody. People are awful like that. Like the guy who was caught last week spreading a boxful of broken glass on the high school football field.

Then again, there are people who mean well, Vera continued, and she told Genesis about the injured blackbird she saw in the street — Vera was maybe ten — and she tried to help it only to startle the bird so much it scampered away and fell down a storm drain.

Vera described the guilt. The dreams she had for weeks. Dreams of cotton candy at the circus. Blackbirds flying around inside the circus tent, so many they looked like black-pepper rain from the sky, and these blackbirds swooped down and picked out the eyes of all the children in the bleachers.

Catfish so big they hung all the way from Dad's belt to the ground. Ten-foot catfish too. Long whiskers, so long they dragged people to the murky, warm lake bottom.

Genesis slid her hood back and looked at Vera. Smoke blew out her nostrils. Her skin was no longer fair and fresh-looking like in the car. It was ruddy now, wrinkles trenching her cheeks and her neck. Her green eyes retreated behind purplish-black bags, and they looked tired. They used to glimmer with energy. Genesis herself used to glimmer with energy, Vera thought, all the time. Her smile used to beam across the room. Now her teeth were yellowish brown.

Time to get moving, Vera thought too. When they were moving, the past six years waned behind, and the clock dialed back. When they were stopped, the clock caught up.

The fog was at its thickest, and the power plant lights were obscured. Vera felt far away and cut off from the world.

A splash, louder and closer than the previous splashes, split the fog, but the source was hidden.

No — there. There!

Thirty feet or so past the shoreline, billowy murk hung like an old man's white hair above what looked to Vera like disturbance rings spreading larger than before.

With her toe, Vera turned over a flat stone. The underside was covered with clumps of damp dirt. A worm wriggled and disappeared down a small hole.

Vera's imagination fired up. A catfish—no, a hundred, maybe a thousand catfish, all bigger than the one her dad caught—will snatch her with their whiskers, wind them around her ankles and wrists, and drag her down, then perhaps up a pipe, steam billowing and scalding, and she'll wail in pain and fear, but the cotton candy will stuff her mouth, mouthful by mouthful as she struggles, and dirty water will flood her throat so that no scream can bubble surfaceward and slice the fog.

Her logical side told her it was not a monstrous catfish surfacing to seize her, and the fog was too thick for skipping stones because the stones would skip out of sight, and where was the fun in that, but she picked up the stone anyway, hefted it—when was the last time she'd done this?—and shied it out and down toward where she'd heard the splash.

...*plish...plish...plish...*

A shrouded voice howled suddenly and deeply as if right in front of them: "Ow!"

"We should go," Vera said, pride in her arm's agility shattered.

The two bolted for the car, and soon they were speeding down the highway. A half mile went by, and the fog lifted to reveal peach-mango light.

"The rain cleared," Vera said.

An odd phenomenon, she knew. The power plant and the lake generated fog so dense and wrinkly you had no idea what the weather was like beyond it.

She wasn't going to bring up throwing the stone. She was confident Genesis wouldn't either. A few miles later, Vera could see Genesis turning youthful again.

Genesis pointed at an ultralight trike landing in the field next to the highway.

Vera pulled over. Why not? Genesis probably hadn't seen anything like that in ages, unless ultralights flew over the prison.

This ultralight was constructed with three aluminum poles that connected to an open fuselage pod with three wheels. The propeller and engine were on the back, and the delta fabric wing was attached above, framed with longer poles that drooped toward the ground near the wingtips when the ultralight wasn't moving.

Genesis opened her door and ran from the car. Her hood flapped behind her. She crossed the field and stopped by the ultralight. She appeared to be speaking to the pilot.

This aroused some envy in Vera. The first words her sister was speaking outside of prison were to a stranger whose face was too far away for Vera to see.

Vera watched, confused, as Genesis climbed behind the pilot. The propeller whirred, the engine buzzed louder, and the ultralight shook and rolled over the field a short ways before lifting off.

It flew for ten minutes in long circles about a thousand feet up. Before it landed, it swooped in low over Vera's car.

Vera hollered and waved.

After the ultralight touched the ground, it bounced in a rut and flipped over.

Vera ran up to the wrecked heap.

The wing fabric was torn.

All propeller blades were broken.

Genesis and the pilot were upside down.

Genesis was unhurt and pulling herself out of the harness holding her into the seat behind the pilot.

The pilot was bleeding from his head. Blood covered his face, and he was groaning and gasping, his arm hanging limply.

Vera called the police, and they came not more than a few minutes later. If Genesis was nervous around the officers, she didn't show it.

But the siren that took the pilot away haunted Vera's dreams for a long time afterward. So did Genesis. When the police were looking the other way taking notes, Genesis grunted and strained and rolled the fuselage pod upright. She situated herself in the pilot's seat and looked encaged by the bent aluminum poles, red and blue prowler lights bedazzling her prison face.

SPÉED
LIMIT
55

SNAKE WINE

EDOARDO APPOLLINO LEANED AGAINST THE
galley sink and held a black Dutch oven under the
faucet. He turned on the water and waited until he had
enough to cook the penne for his ex-wife. The Dutch oven
grew heavier as it filled. Edoardo shut the water off and
tipped the Dutch oven. Excess water spilled into the sink.

"Don't fill it up all the way," Billie, his ex-wife, said from
the forward cabin of Edoardo's 32-foot boat.

"I like feeling it get heavier," Edoardo said, and it was
true—the weight of water was the only measure by which he
knew he was still living.

"Feel it get heavier without filling it up all the way."

Edoardo slid the Dutch oven onto the small stove. It
scraped on the burner. Two pinches of salt. A spritz of gas
puffed into flame.

"Wasteful," Billie said again.

Edoardo looked at her from the galley. She was leaning
backward on the worn, vinyl-covered lounge seat, and her
legs were splayed out with her bare feet up on his sofa

sleeper across from her. Her black leggings were too tight, and her green cable-knit sweater was too big. The green polish on her toenails was flaking.

A guinea pig sat like a puffy ascot on her chest. Its head was buried in her hair, which came down past her neck in a sweeping pile of dark blond curls. The animal made suction-like slurping noises while it gnawed on her sweater's neckline.

"Couple minutes until boiling," Edoardo said.

The guinea pig grunted and squeaked. Billie reached into a bowl on the end table for a piece of carrot. The animal snatched it from her fingers and buried its head back in her curls to make crunching noises now.

"Carrots, parrots," Billie said to the guinea pig. She puckered her lips at it. The guinea pig kept chewing.

It was a black guinea pig. Its hair stuck out in all directions in bowl-like loops and ringlets on its back. Edoardo was disgusted at the bald patches in the center of them.

Why did she bring the damn thing, he thought.

He ignited the second burner, turned the flame down low, and put on a small, covered pan of leftover red sauce.

"It's going to snow pretty bad," he said to Billie. "Maybe you should call a motel and see if you can get a room tonight."

Billie lay down on the lounge seat. She cradled her arm around the guinea pig so it wouldn't fall. From the round window above her, the dim, damp light from thick, gray clouds of late autumn low over the lakeshore shaded the hollows of her face, and she looked old in that light, tired. The wrinkles around her eyes were knife scratches on a weathered barn wall.

"Just raining," she said.

"Supposed to freeze. Then snow."

"Early in the year for that kind of weather," she said.

Steam feathers skated on the smooth water in the Dutch oven.

Edoardo took two plates from a cabinet and placed them opposite each other on the fold-down table. He set silverware and two wine glasses next to the plates, and a Parmigiano-Reggiano triangle and a stainless-steel grater. He tore off two pieces from a paper towel roll, folded them, and put them on the table too.

He sat on the sofa sleeper across from Billie in the cramped forward cabin that was cozy with heat from a bulkhead space heater. On all the faux-teak plank walls hung photos of himself with the assistant district attorney, the governor, the secretary of commerce, the producer in California who created a show about terrorists and torture, all people he had once known. Those not dead were no doubt heavier now. Edoardo hadn't seen them in years. He sometimes thought ahead to when he'd only exist in someone else's pictures, like young grandparents in their silver-framed sepia wedding portraits on the nightstand of a granddaughter now grown, divorced, and wondering how and when she too got old, until Edoardo remembered no one had pictures of him.

"No such thing as too early in the year," he said to Billie. "They say it's going to be a hard winter."

"What are you going to do?" Billie said.

"Stay here."

"Can you?"

"Hope so."

"What about when the water freezes?"

"Big lake. Maybe it won't."

Half a mahogany wheel from an old ship hung above the space heater. The wheel was five feet wide and took up the entire bulkhead. Edoardo had found it broken, four of its spokes missing, behind a dumpster by the ice cream shack, but he'd brought it to the boat anyway, scoured the brass hub, and polished the wood to a new sheen.

Maybe it won't.

Edoardo was pushing his luck keeping the boat inside the breakwater so late in the fall, but the folks in charge of the marina hadn't told him to move it out, so perhaps he had time.

There was no house. The boat was his only place. He'd been living in it since May, when he returned from Lamma Island. He and Billie had once upon a time taken the boat out on Lake Michigan together, with their daughter, every summer weekend back when they were still married, and the boat was cheaper than renting or buying, two things Edoardo couldn't afford now, most of his money gone. Living on his boat was a better option than selling it.

"They store boats here — on land — for the winter," Edoardo said. "Might be possible to rent a spot with a hook-up. Could prop up a ladder for in and out."

Billie continued making kissing sounds at the guinea pig.

Edoardo wasn't sure if she'd heard him. He didn't care so he went through the galley and up the short set of stairs to the top, barefoot in spite of the cold, where he lit a cigarette on the helm chair. The helm chair was open to the air and water, and Edoardo liked it that way. Out on the lake, there was nothing better than wind lashing his hair and spray whipping his face. Some afternoons, a yacht from the yacht club crawled across the marina and roared out into the open lake—Edoardo would stare after its enclosed wheelhouse and throw his cigarette butt in the direction the boat had gone.

Get your hair messed up in the wind a little, he'd think.

He'd keep staring at the boat's wash as it left the marina. It would curve as the boat turned, and Edoardo would imagine it was a kite line holding the yacht to shore. Many afternoons, he drank too much wine, and the powerful propellers tugged at the line, unreeling it fast, and Edoardo grabbed it before it played out, cut it quick with a broken bottle neck, and flew behind the yacht, higher and higher, line tied around his waist and his arms stretched like wings, until land was gone. The rare afternoons without wine, its roar would only hover over the lake. He'd watch the ladies holding onto their hats in the wind and wish he was with them. The hats would disappear, and pretty soon the yacht too would fall past the horizon, its swells racing to join waves and its wash bubbling flat.

Edoardo inhaled. Blew out. The knife-cold wind off the lake erased the smoke as soon as it left his mouth. Edoardo faced the wind and watched the clouds bringing in a dark veil that swept the water ahead of freezing snow.

A few sailboats still bobbed at their moorings. Their masts swung back and forth. Dark was falling, and lights behind windows in town turned on. A flag on shore flapped.

Someone was walking a dog on the beach. The dog darted in and out of the water like a needle threading through thick wool.

Edoardo finished his cigarette and threw the butt over the side. His fingers were stiffening. His toes were throbbing with cold. His heart was a magician's hat, and the heaviness in it was a long rag that kept coming and coming out of it. He couldn't stuff the rag back in, and he couldn't pull it all the way out.

Edoardo stayed up top for ten more minutes.

"Water's boiling," he heard Billie call from below.

He went back down and dropped a pound of dried penne in the Dutch oven. Steam pillowcases burst in his face, but they felt good after outside. He rubbed his hands in the steam and inhaled some. After he stirred the sauce and covered it, there was nothing to do but sit on the sofa sleeper.

Billie was still on the lounge seat with the guinea pig.

"What's his name?" Edoardo said.

"Arnie."

"Arnie, the guinea pig." Dumb name, like a drive-in root beer stand with a fat short-order cook in a dirty apron.

"What?" Billie said.

"Interesting name."

"You don't like it?"

"Didn't say that."

"It rhymes with Ailie," she said. She smiled.

Edoardo didn't return it.

"What's wrong?" she said. She stopped petting the guinea pig. Her smile deflated to a frown.

Edoardo looked away from her and at the brass hub of the

wheel. Someday the nails it hangs on, he thought, will bend under its weight, and it will crash to the floor.

"Motel?" he said.

The round window above the lounge seat was dark. Rainwater now trickled down the other side of the glass.

Edoardo thought about what his boat might look like from outside. A little boat, bobbing in the wind with its small, round windows all lit up, surrounded by a lattice of cozy light from its windows and cold sleet. Vast night behind it. In the dark, boats looked much smaller and the water much bigger, but Edoardo was convinced it wasn't just a matter of appearances. Light restrained water, made it hum like a stretched string, and in the absence of it, when it was night, water rose on its two hind legs with a roar.

"Can't we take the boat out for a ride?" Billie said.

Edoardo looked at her. "Not good in a storm."

"Is the storm going to be bad?"

"Winter storms could sink us in two seconds flat."

Shipwrecks on the Great Lakes fascinated Edoardo, and he liked talking about them. He liked shipwrecks in the oceans too, but those of the Great Lakes were more haunting, more mysterious. They could fill his lungs, pull him under, make him feel closer to the bottom, weightless.

"Winter storms on Lake Michigan," he continued, "have been known to be worse than those on the North Atlantic."

Billie's eyebrows went up. "Really?" she said.

"They come out of nowhere, without warning. First come big waves that crash over the bow, over the stern. Any boat caught broadside is in trouble. It isn't strong enough for that kind of punishment, even if its bow is pointed in the wind.

The up and down of the waves, the crashing of the water. Like a mugger beating down an old lady for her purse."

Billie glowered at Edoardo.

He enjoyed how his description seemed to bother her. "All this water collects on the decks and overloads the boat. It rides too low. More water comes spilling everywhere. The worst part is when this water freezes. The ice stays there, making the boat dangerously unstable. It becomes top heavy. The wind rolls it over. All the men on it go into the cold water. Even if they make it to a lifeboat and launch it in time, there's no way it'll survive out there. Think if a big steel boat can't survive, how can a little wooden one?"

Edoardo made large circles and waves in the air with his hands while he talked and sound effects to drive home a ship breaking up in a storm.

"Like the *Edmund Fitzgerald*?" Billie said.

"She broke apart in a November storm. Hurricane-force."

Billie was petting the guinea pig again. "If you want to drown so badly," she said, "why don't you just do it?" Her cheek was on the guinea pig's fur.

The animal was back to chewing her neckline.

"Carrying a load of taconite on Lake Superior," Edoardo said. "She disappeared from the surface so fast the men on her didn't have time to make a distress call."

Edoardo stopped. He had no response for Billie's question. He'd tried to drown but couldn't by himself, and fate was not kind to him. It refused to throw him a circumstance in which the water would take him. But there outside the window above Billie, the bow of the *Fitzgerald* knifed up over a swell and crashed down in a blast of spray.

The ship rolled in the wind like a newspaper hat. Her men shouted while scrambling to save her. A sailor was washed overboard, and he screamed, and the storm swallowed the scream as if he never lived.

Like the rip current, Edoardo thought.

His boat rocked. It knocked softly on the dock-edge fenders.

"Could that happen to us?" Billie said.

Edoardo nodded. His lungs itched for another cigarette. His head was in need of wine. He went to the galley.

Billie followed him. She placed the guinea pig gently on the fold-down table. It chewed on one of the paper towels.

Edoardo opened the cabinet and pulled out a squat, pyramid-shaped bottle filled with yellow wine and a coiled cobra.

Billie took it from him. "Chinese letters on the label," she said. "What's that inside?" She turned the bottle around and held it up to the light. Then she shrieked and dropped it.

Edoardo was fast. He caught it before it hit the floor.

Billie leaned away from him, eyes wide and hands out. "Jesus fuck," she said.

The cobra's hood swayed in the wine, and its coiled body settled like a spring.

"Where did you get it?" she said.

"Hong Kong."

She pointed dramatically at Edoardo. "We are not drinking that." Her lips quivered, and her voice shook. She put her hand on her forehead and blinked many times.

"It's quite good," Edoardo said. "I've been saving the last bottle for a special occasion."

"We are not drinking that." She sat and hid her face with her hands.

Edoardo set the bottle on the table.

Billie turned away from it.

He sat down too.

The cobra coiled inside the bottle was a murky swamp color, gray and black and green. It swayed some more with the wine's motion as Edoardo slid the bottle across the table toward Billie. The guinea pig bumped its nose on the bottle and sniffed it. It tried to chew off a corner of the label.

"Put that someplace where I don't have to look at it," Billie said.

Edoardo put it on the floor under the table.

"You're not drinking that in front of me," she said.

"I got it at a night market," he said. "Lots of fake stuff there. Knock-off clothes, leather, cameras, watches."

Billie groaned and said, from behind her hands, "That better be a knock-off snake."

"Tiny liquor store down a crowded alley by the market. Had snake wine, mouse embryo wine, lizard wine."

The liquor store's entrance was tucked between two stands, one a fruit stand and the other a fish stand. Edoardo almost walked right past it without seeing it. But he did see it—the dark entrance was an obsidian slab leaning against the buildings.

The fruit and fish stands were Xiamen tigers. The night air in the alley was muggy, clung to his skin, smelled of garbage, sweat, and garlic. Edoardo was standing before a cave, and the tigers were guarding it. The cave's interior pulled him. The tigers ignored him as he walked in, as if they knew he expected them to pounce on him and rip him to bloody pieces.

Inside the cave, people scurried unseen in the dark. Their shoes slapped the rocky floor. Their voices chattered and echoed. Water trickled somewhere, probably from a drainpipe leading from a building into a sewer.

He walked, feeling his way inch by inch with his toes. Deep inside, after inching for a long time with his hands out before him, the trickling of a faraway subterranean river guided him, and little by little it became louder until he was upon it and it was a roaring cascade he could not see. The sounds of people scurrying were now sounds of people slipping on rock and falling in the river.

Edoardo's eyes adjusted after he stood there a long time. Ahead of him was a long black tunnel.

He was moving. He was on a skiff. He sat down because the skiff was rocking and he was afraid of losing his balance, falling in that river. The skiff bumped the rock walls and knocked into other boats on the river, but as it gained speed it stayed in the center. It shot Edoardo down the tunnel, winding through twists and curves, occasionally scraping the cave's walls.

"Why do they drink the stuff?" Billie said.

"Serpents have curative powers," he said. He held up the bottle. "A good fall drink. A healing agent for the body. Drives away chills."

"Put it away."

"Why?"

"I don't want to look at it."

"Why does it scare you?"

Billie took her hands from her face and looked at him. "The snake will jump out when you open the bottle. It might bite me."

"It's dead."

"Even dead snakes can bite."

Edoardo got up and put the bottle back in the cabinet. He stirred the penne boiling on the stove. He stirred the sauce and put the cover back on.

Billie sighed.

Edoardo sat down again. "When you go through the gate, turn left. There's a motel a mile down, next to the gas station. No need to leave now, but soon as we get done eating, before the roads ice up."

"These last few years have just been so hard," Billie said. "When you stayed there and I came home without you, and you never came home, it was like you'd died too."

Edoardo had expected her to say this because she often spoke expected, predictable things.

"I didn't know if you were ever coming back," she said.

When he did, it wasn't for Billie or the boat. The sea hadn't wanted Edoardo, but maybe the lake would. He would have stayed on Lamma Island forever otherwise, walking Hung Shing Yeh Beach at night, venturing in the ocean at exactly five minutes after ten, lingering at first at water's edge while the sea tasted his toes and grabbed his ankles, hearing in his memory how Billie's voice had once said, a lifetime ago, *Go on in, honey, but only a little ways, not too far in the dark.* His mouth tingled with the aftertaste of yellow curry and cayenne, just like that night. His head swam with the boozy vapors of too much wine, just like that night. Deeper he went, slowly because the water felt cold to him, though it was warm, and he rocked unsteady in the shifting sand deepening under his heels. Hands at his sides. He turned around in circles a few times on account of the boozy vapors directing him by the shoulders until the sea was up to his chest and the waves lifted him off the bottom and carried him out.

In the morning, he woke shivering on the sand by the rocks. Every time. It was a ritual he repeated his entire stay on Lamma Island because he wasn't afraid. When it became clear the sea was stubborn and his money was almost gone, he had no choice but to come home to nothing. But he hadn't started the ritual with the lake, though the lake's water seemed heavier, because its lack of salt scared him, and, with no sting in his sinuses and no burn in his throat, he couldn't go in above his head.

"Dinner should be ready soon," he said.

Billie put her face in her hands again.

The serpent in the bottle was alive. Edoardo knew and didn't tell her. It was a magic serpent that possessed the power to slither through the glass of the bottle and varnished wood cabinets as easily as through a cascade of water. It coiled and suspended in the air, floated behind Billie's head, its hood swaying, and struck at her neck. She gasped and fell to the floor. She jerked once, twice, convulsed several more times, mouth open. The fear in her eyes gave way to curtains of relief, like a sigh. The snake looked down on her, its hood still extended and tongue flickering. Billie's chin, cheeks, lips, and eyes soon oozed a purplish-black pus, and her skin bloated so fast it split. While Billie was dying, the snake writhed around Edoardo's forearm, and when she gasped and jerked one last time, wine bottles shining in her dead eyes, the snake betrayed Edoardo and struck his neck too.

Billie started crying. She leaned back in her chair and brushed away her tears. She picked up the guinea pig from the table and held it. She rocked back and forth, making kissing noises and rubbing her cheek on its fur.

"You should go," Edoardo said. Drinking, when he drank, was his time. Open bottle. Yellow burning down his throat. Cobra's company.

Billie continued rocking the guinea pig.

"You should go," he said a little louder.

Billie stopped rocking. "I need to use the bathroom," she said. She stood. "Hold Arnie."

The bathroom was just two steps from the table. Billie entered it the way one enters an airplane lavatory, backwards, eyes to the floor. The door clicked shut.

The guinea pig's fur brushed Edoardo's neck. It was prickly, and it tickled. The animal climbed up higher on his chest and nibbled his ear. It wasn't a painful nibble, but it was annoying.

The water in the Dutch oven boiled over.

Bubbles rose above the rim and spilled down the sides.

Steam hissed up from the flame.

Edoardo jumped from the table and slid the Dutch oven onto the cool center of the stove, but the Dutch oven's hot handles scalded his palms. He yelled and flapped his hands.

The guinea pig slid off him. Its little claws clung to his shirt, but it kept sliding.

Edoardo grabbed for it, but it fell into the boiling Dutch

oven.

Hot water drops splashed Edoardo's hands and face and stung him.

The guinea pig let out a shrill scream just before it went under the water.

Penne overflowed and rolled to the floor. It burned the tops of Edoardo's bare feet, and he danced.

The guinea pig leaped all the way out of the Dutch oven and landed on the covered sauce pot.

The pot spilled, sauce splattered on the wall, the cover bounced to the floor, and the guinea pig scurried around on the stove, shrieking and leaving wet trails.

It brushed the hissing, popping open flame and hopped again. It flew up in an arc above the Dutch oven.

One long scream.

The guinea pig reached the top of its arc, hung for a split second, and fell.

Edoardo tried again to catch it, but it dropped down the narrow space between the stove and the wall, smearing the sauce. Its body thumped the floor.

From behind the closed bathroom door came noises like someone struggling to zip up.

Edoardo turned off both flames, bent down, and pulled out the dead guinea pig. It was still hot but not too hot to handle. Its hair was dripping water, matted with sauce, and covered in dust balls from the floor. Its tongue lolled from its mouth. Edoardo held it. He looked into its blank eyes.

Why did she bring the damn thing?

He was looking in the eyes of the men on the *Fitzgerald*. The men were on the cold lake bottom, trapped, their last horrible howls of fear frozen on their faces. Their eyes were wide. Scavengers had not yet begun to nibble them from the sockets.

He should have been feeling grief all this time, but he hadn't been. Now it made sense why. His had been pulled out with Ailie by the typhoon-stirred rip current on Hung Shing Yeh Beach — the typhoon had been hundreds of miles past the horizon, but its long, slender, death-beckoning fingers reached underwater all the way to the coast — and no matter how many times he went in the ocean to join her, her gray, saltwater-bloated body eluded him, and the seas retuned him to the shore as if it didn't fucking matter that he wanted to be a body too. But he couldn't consider giving up, and maybe the water of the lake would reward him. It felt heavier, after all, colder. If only he could get past the lack of salt.

The bathroom door popped open. Billie looked at the guinea pig in Edoardo's arms and then looked at Edoardo. Her hand flew up to her mouth. She scooped the guinea pig up with the other and held it close. She looked at Edoardo again.

"What killed it?" she said softly, her eyes wide. "Was it the snake?"

It had been several snakes.

When Edoardo's skiff on the underground river in the cave had come to a bend and lodged between two rocks at the water's edge, Edoardo stepped out and followed an amber light up a sloping passageway.

At the passageway's end, he emerged in a brilliantly lit room. His eyes didn't need to adjust to the light. A shelf from floor to ceiling held rows of pyramid-shaped bottles filled with coiled cobras and yellow wine. He picked up two, cradled them in the crook of each arm, paid, and walked from the liquor store into the alley and past the Xiamen tigers that were in the next moment a fruit stand and a fish stand.

Before he left China, he shipped a crate home, and it cruised through customs uninspected.

Billie shoved the guinea pig in her purse. She slid on her shoes and put on her coat. She walked up the short stairs to the top without saying another word. Her shoes echoed on the dock's planks. The sound faded and disappeared.

He pictured her walking alone on the beach toward her car. She kicked up sand as she walked, and her warm tears mixed with the freezing rain. Her arms pumped back and forth, and her purse swung on its strap.

It would be the last time he thought of her.

He went up to the helm chair. He listened to the wind roar in. Sand-like snow gritted his face. Rain froze in his hair. He lit a cigarette and stared out over the large lake that grew larger at night. He felt safer than he had in a long time. He made up his mind to untie the ropes, start up the engine, and head out as soon as his cigarette was done to locate the creaks and groans of the *Fitzgerald* rolling in the waves and to sound for the terror of her men, home in on their cries, map the grief of the wives and children they'd left behind on shore.

Maybe he'd stay out there for a few days and drift around. He estimated he had enough food to do that for a week. Long enough to reach Lake Superior perhaps. It didn't matter that it would be cold out there. He'd be warm enough inside his boat.

The lake would be kind to him.

SPEED LIMIT 55

MOXIE IS ENOUGH

"IF WE HAD A CAT," the newlywed wife says from the passenger seat, "Moxie wouldn't be lonely while we're at work."

The black Pomeranian is sitting in her lap smiling, its tongue out and ears up. It looks back and forth out the windshield and out the side window.

The newlywed husband scratches the dog's ear before he reverses the car and backs down the red-dirt driveway. His arm is sore, so he shifts his grip. His new tattoo is swollen and oozy — a sticky layer of Aquaphor casts a shiny reflection on the windshield above the steering wheel. His arm is stiff because he always holds it up in a way that keeps the Aquaphor from rubbing on his shirt.

His wife has a habit of nagging him when Aquaphor rubs on his shirt because then she has to spray Zout on it, which is an extra inconvenient step.

The husband brakes near the mailbox and thinks about jumping out quick. Clovis Pope's second novel — first edition, first printing — is due to arrive today, according to the post office tracking he checked online earlier, but he wants to hurry along to the bookstore for another favorite author's new release.

So he continues backing into the street after looking both ways. He watches the mailbox in the rearview mirror shrink in the distance as he foots some speed in the wheels. Is it too hot out, he wonders, to leave the book there for another hour? Assuming it has come?

The sun is bright in that gauzy way he's only seen in Georgia. It shines in through his side window and makes his raw arm resting straight along the door sill feel like pinpricks rolling all over on it, up and down, but the husband is proud of what a nice tattoo it is of a long palm tree that stretches from elbow to wrist, palm fronds wrapping around his upper forearm.

The dog lies down in the wife's lap once the car is underway. She licks her paws. Her front toenails are painted red to match the newlywed wife's.

"A pawdicure," the newlywed wife usually calls it.

He thinks it's a waste of money. He said so the first time she brought the dog home from the doggie salon, which she refers to as the paw spa. This was two years before they were married. She continued to get the dog's nails done regardless.

He thought then and still thinks now that the dog's painted toenails look like Barbie shoes. Sometimes he worries the polish will flake off and the dog will ingest the flakes, but he figures if the paw spa uses it, then it must be safe for dogs.

The dog's licking soon plants a wet spot on the wife's pants. Wet spots are nothing out of the ordinary for the husband and the wife because the dog always sits in their laps and licks her paws.

If she is irked at his avoidance of the cat suggestion, the wife doesn't show it.

But he is irked at the cat suggestion. Nevertheless, he lets it go and brakes for a red light. The tires thump on the asphalt.

The black Pomeranian puts her head down and closes her eyes.

The intersection boasts four churches leaning like gravestones, one church on each corner. The red light glares. In the minute or so before it turns green, the husband wonders, because he hates his job and often fantasizes about a different one, how good his chances are of getting elected in Georgia. In that short time sitting there, he runs an entire campaign—primary to general election to runoff—in his mind, a campaign in which his strategy involves a fake Georgia drawl, a smile like he has octopus tentacles for lips and teeth, a pickup to round up illegals in, and a teenage boy to wave a gun at.

Run as a right-winger to get elected. Vote far left once in the Capitol. That might be fun. Fooling the voters.

Pretending to be Christian guarantees a win, he reminds himself.

"Why are the tires making that noise?" the wife says.

The light turns green, and the husband lead-foots it, pushes the churches behind, whips ahead along a steady line of political signs that pass by fast on each side of the street.

"We need new ones soon." He is worried about where they will find the money for them. They charged several thousand dollars a few weeks ago at a resort in Cartagena, which still annoys the husband because he hoped they would receive enough cash to pay for the whole honeymoon. Except for a few checks from his family in Boston, they received piles and stacks of gifts, all from the local kitchen wares boutique, which won't accept returns without a receipt. Hand-painted plates. Hand-carved wooden bowls. Vine-patterned casserole dishes. Matching lids. Wrought-iron stands for round display plaques with their names stenciled on them.

Mr. & Mrs.

Much of it is packed away at the wife's grandmother's house. On the bright side, the husband concedes, he can go over to the wife's grandmother's house any time he's tired of his wine glasses and wants new ones.

The bookstore parking lot is wide open. The dog perks up and wriggles around. The husband parks and kills the car. The temperature in it immediately begins rising.

"Anyway," he says, "we probably should not have gone to Cartagena."

The wife rolls her eyes and play-punches the husband's arm.

He is still thinking about his campaign fantasy when he leaves her and the dog at a table outside the coffee shop next door and enters the bookstore.

He scans the new arrivals spines. His annoyance ticks up a notch when he finds out the new Olive Evelyn book he wants is already in a second printing. He picks up each copy and flips to the copyright page. A first printing is nowhere on the shelf.

The wife is waiting outside with Moxie. Moxie is relaxing under the café chair the wife is sitting in, but she is panting hard because her fur is long and thick. Wet spots dot the sidewalk around her. Her last haircut was only a month ago, but her fur grows fast and fluffy.

"Did they have the Olive Eleven book?" the wife says.

"They did," the husband says, "but it was a second printing." He wants to tell his wife the way she deliberately misspeaks is annoying rather than cute, but he doesn't tell her that.

All the other tables are empty like the parking lot. The strip mall is dead today.

"I'm sorry," she says. "Maybe we should look for it at Bare Knees & Knob Lee."

In the moment between the husband finishing his sentence about the second printing and his wife's Bare Knees & Knob Lee response, the husband has written an entire novel in his head about an apocalypse sparked by ocean pollution that he, his wife, and their dog are the only survivors of due to an unexplained immunity.

The fear of apocalypse, of being alone in the world, and of being married to this woman who claims to love him is small, but it drops from the back of his mouth to his stomach and tightens so quickly it's gone before he understands it.

Just as quickly, he forgets the novel he has written in his head. He forgets it because they are both young, with the vast plain of their lives together stretching to the horizon and beyond, and who will help them out if they're the last two people in the world?

And the way she mispronounces store names too is not that cute. The husband worries she hasn't yet revealed a habit of saying aminals, crinimals, supposably, misunderestimate, and nuke-you-lar.

"I didn't think it would be in a second printing already," he says.

"I know how much you like Olive Elephant," she says.

"Moxie is sleepy," he says.

"Did she work a shift at McMoxie's this morning?"

"She did. She says it was hot. The air conditioner was broken."

Moxie looks up at him and smiles and pants.

"Sure is hot for October," the wife says.

"Moxie says she had to throw out a Chihuahua and a Dalmatian for fighting over a dropped Purina burger."

The wife laughs. Moxie stands and turns around in a circle a few times. She jumps up on her back legs and paws at the husband's knees.

"Okay, okay," the husband tells the dog. He squats and rubs both sides of her face. She licks his wrist, the red and puffy one, where a yellow-bellied sea snake coils at the palm tree's base.

He flinches because her tongue is like a flame.

"Remember when the other dogs at McMoxie's made fun of her," the wife says, "when she told them we give her tomatoes and lettuce and blueberries sometimes?"

"They're just jealous they don't eat as well as Moxie does," the husband says.

The stories they make up about the dog give him a modest sense of enjoyment. The newlywed husband and wife began telling these stories a year or so ago after they first moved in together to satisfy their curiosity about what Moxie did when they were at work. Moxie was curled asleep on the bathmat by the tub, but as time went on and the stories grew, it was more fun to believe Moxie was off on grand adventures.

Moxie escaped from their house through a secret tunnel behind the bathroom sink. She hit up the neighbors' houses to mooch Virginia Slims from the neighbor pooches, also living it up home alone.

She started her own business, McMoxie's, the best dog diner in town, known for its juicy Purina burgers. The Old West-style saloon swinging doors were customers' favorite part of the place. Moxie threw out roughhouse mutts that drooled all over her sawdust floors or, because they hadn't yet been fixed, growled too wolfishly at the pink toy-poodle waitresses prancing around to the plunk-plunk notes from the rinky-tink piano in the corner.

Moxie typed her memoirs in the afternoon once the lunch rush died down.

She mixed herself lemon-drop martinis.

"The pet store has a new litter of kittens," the wife says.

The husband sighs at his wife, who is looking up at him as if she knows what his answer will be but is compelled to ask anyway. It is a mixed look of defiance and pleading.

An image of a woodpecker comes to both their minds at the same time. He resents her for being a little woodpecker drilling away at his sense of order and control. She is pleased with herself for being persistent.

The husband realizes it's a trap. He wants to stop at the pet store to exchange the Halloween costume they bought last week. Moxie needs a smaller size. The costume they bought falls to the side and drags while she walks.

He and his wife argued about the costume, of course. She felt it took away Moxie's sense of dignity.

He felt it was something fun to do.

She countered that Moxie deserved better than to perform circus tricks in a clumsy taco costume.

He said people dressed their dogs in costumes all the time.

Besides, he added, she didn't have a problem spending money on toenail polish.

Halloween is his favorite holiday, but it's been years since he's worn a costume or passed out candy. The last time he wore a costume, he broke his ankle wearing stilettos so high he teetered, grabbed the towel rack, ripped it out the wall, and crashed into the tub, his ankle bent one way and his leg bent the other, one shoe's heel snapped in half. His make-up smeared the bottom of the tub, and he went to the emergency room with his face swollen and bruised.

Other than ocean adventure novels by Clovis Pope and Olive Evelyn, and sometimes Kenny Loggins songs turned up as loud as they can go, his pop culture diet consists primarily of freaks, monsters, children of the night, killers, and, though you will never convince him he should believe in them, ghosts.

Who doesn't love a good ghost story? he thinks.

But he hasn't worn a costume in a while now. That's okay—Halloween is still his favorite holiday because he enjoys watching others enjoy it and feels their dog should enjoy it just as much as he does.

But the wife knows they're going to the pet store to exchange the costume, and she wants a kitten.

"Moxie is enough," the husband says.

The wife turns her chin down and scratches Moxie's back. She lately has been trying to see the world from the dog's point of view, a world she imagines is black and white with fuzzy and shadowy edges.

In the car again, the wife studies her husband while he maneuvers past the payment machine and the boom gate at the car wash. While she is impressed with how he combs his hair so that not a single strand is out of place, how he irons and starches his shirts so that he gives the impression he's going to the office even on a Saturday, and how the determination in his eyes and in his jaw pushes him to wash and vacuum his car every day as if he's someone's chauffeur, she also seeks clues in his demeanor that will help her understand where his meticulousness comes from.

Blue and green foam squiggles down the windshield. The side brushes spin, and the car lurches toward the waltzing vertical blinds that bring back fond recital memories for the wife because they remind her of the curtain that parted when it was her turn to tap dance out on stage.

The dog's tongue, pink like taffy, dangles and drips. The dog concentrates on the car wash going by like it's a psychedelic trip.

The wife half listens to her husband complain about the finance manager at work, who doesn't understand the concept of foreign currency and exchange rates. She knows he is stressing about it because he doesn't want the finance manager to discover that his conference in Cartagena was also their honeymoon.

"I had to send several emails last week explaining that the amounts on my receipts didn't match the amounts on my expense report because the receipts were in Columbian pesos and the expense items were in dollars," he says. "Then she wanted to know how I arrived at my calculations."

The colors and noises and water carry the wife back to the open-air Cartagena market she spent an afternoon at while the husband was in a meeting. She is sure the expense report will work out fine. He did go to the conference, after all. Best to let him complain, and he'll get over it.

The horn honking breaks her self-distraction. The black Lincoln ahead is at the end, but it is not driving out. Their car approaches closer and closer, and the husband leans longer on the horn.

"Move!" he yells, and he blasts the horn again.

The dog tenses in her lap.

The windows shake from the blowers, and the two cars meet with a knock and a jolt, their front bumper thunking the Lincoln's rear bumper. Their car's back wheel rises up over the roller in the track and drops back down.

The car wash rattles to a stop.

"Give it some gas," the wife says.

The dog jumps off her lap and sits in the footwell.

The husband swears a blue streak. He nudges the Lincoln out by shifting from neutral to drive and egging the pedal.

The black Lincoln continues rolling across the apron, down the incline, and into traffic.

Brakes squeal, horns shriek, and half a dozen cars veer around it.

ELDERLY PRIEST SUFFERS ANEURISM IN TIDAL WAVE WASH, the wife imagines the headlines will say. She assumes an elderly priest would drive a black Lincoln, and she's sure she's seen that black Lincoln parked at Precious Blood outside town. She doesn't know anyone who goes to that church, but every time she passes by she studies an aspect she hasn't before. The cross on top the bell tower. The white marble Virgin statue. The stained-glass windows that look like gas sheens on puddles when the afternoon sun hits them.

The husband puts their car in park. He leaps out and runs toward the Lincoln.

The wife stays in the car and watches through the windshield.

When the husband reaches the Lincoln, its brake lights brighten and turn off, and its left blinker flashes. It drives away, slowly at first as if inching forward at a red light, and then zooms off.

The husband halts, but his tattooed arm still reaches out for where the Lincoln's door handle was. He glances around and runs his hand through his hair.

In no time at all, the car wash attendants reach him. Traffic backs up because they are in the middle of the road. They talk for a minute, all of them looking north in the direction the Lincoln has gone.

Horns in both directions start tooting, so the car wash attendants wave apologetically at the backup and return to work while the husband approaches their car and studies the front end.

"No damage," he says after he gets in.

"That sure was strange," the wife says.

"Whoever that man was," the husband says, "he sure was a fucking moron."

The wife refrains from suggesting that maybe the black Lincoln had a good reason for whatever happened. Nobody got hurt. All's well that ends well.

She is happy to be married, happier than she's been since she can't remember when. Moxie the dog is a perfect addition to their little family too, she thinks, and every year she celebrates her Gotcha Day with a frosted dog cookie while hoping for more additions and more Gotcha Days.

Moxie's first night at home, when she finally fell asleep after a couple hours pacing room to room, was the first time the wife felt as if she no longer needed to hurt herself. Moxie was asleep on her side in bed with her. This pleased the wife because she read that a dog asleep on its side means it feels safe.

She felt safe too. She didn't superglue her fingers together that night like she did every now and then when her need for pain flared up. She was too squeamish for cutting — hospital shows made her nauseous because Hollywood scalpels and skin and incisions and blood looked too real, but gluing her fingers together and ripping them apart was satisfactory. She glued her thumb tip to her index fingertip first, squeezed them together, and separated them as quickly as she could. Sometimes she needed a butter knife to pry them apart or her teeth to gnaw them loose. She next glued her thumb tip to her middle fingertip and so on until all ten fingers blazed blood.

She has no intention to ever tell her husband about it. She knows what he'll say. She reminds herself too that the husband is really the addition to the family because he came along after Moxie.

The sullen cashier at the pet store exchanges the taco costume for a smaller one, which is a relief to the wife because she has been worrying about an argument, but she is disappointed the store has no kittens to look at, just empty cages.

The husband dresses the dog in the new costume before he gets behind the wheel. The dog sits in the wife's lap, and the wife feels sorry for it because the costume makes it pant harder.

"Sure is hot for October," the wife says.

The tires run over something in the road, first the front tire and then the back, and the two quick thumps sound to the wife like a heartbeat.

"What was that?" she says.

"A copperhead, I think," the husband says. "It was stretched out, its head up. Two feet long, I'd guess."

"Did you kill it?" the wife says.

"Believe so."

Trunk or Treat at the wife's church is crowded by the time they arrive. Minivans and sport utility vehicles are lined up across the church parking lot. Hatchbacks are up. Doors are open. Cotton spiderwebs cloak the cars, and plastic jack-o'-lanterns crown them like cupolas.

An animatronic vampire near a maroon van holds the Ten Commandments. First it holds them this way. Then it turns them that way. Its eyes flash crimson.

Propped on a card table next to a growling Frankenstein bust, a plywood speech balloon praises Jesus.

"Frankenstein's *monster*," the wife has heard her husband correct people in the past, and she's willing to bet he'll say something today if anyone calls the bust Frankenstein.

Several folks pass out candy. They are in costume. Clowns. Dorothys. Witches. A mummy. A skeleton. A few evil butlers.

The dog's taco costume attracts a lot of attention. Children and their grabbing hands. Parents and their cameras.

The dog knows she's a star. Her taffy tongue is a royal greeting.

The wife, however, suddenly feels like coming unglued. Too many people. Too hot. Brass band too loud. She is flustered because the dog shouldn't be this tolerant of the blubbering tubas and yawping trombones.

Mr. and Mrs. Rainwater, in Raggedy Ann and Andy costumes, appear from nowhere and faun over the dog. Shrill baby talk.

Mrs. Rainwater straightens. Her say-cheese smile looks like crumbled sharp cheddar. Bad blood squinches her eyes because the wife hasn't been seen in church lately. The wife knows that's what it is. Mrs. Rainwater couldn't be more transparent with that big fake smile and self-righteous eyes.

The wife's mother and father have stopped nagging about Sundays, but they still expect that she and her husband will at least drop by for special occasions like Trunk or Treat. Or else, the wife's mother has a habit of saying, "What *will* people think?" People like Mrs. Rainwater.

"Be careful by the bounce house," Mrs. Rainwater says. "The kids are dropping chocolate over there. They don't pick it up. Best keep your dog away."

Mr. Rainwater says something to the husband about the election next week.

"We need to do what we can to preserve tax-exempt status for churches," the husband says.

That he would say something like this out of the blue surprises the wife. It wasn't that long ago he told her that churches should be taxed to pay for universal health care. The wife hates politics to begin with, so she leads the dog in another direction and walks her across the parking lot. She doesn't want to stick around to hear how that conversation goes.

Near the Styrofoam graveyard, word catches up to the wife. She is halfway to her parents' van, where her mother has promised to hand out peanut butter cups and bubblegum pops. Annual tradition.

The pastor's wife overtakes her from behind and blocks her way. "Your husband!"

The wife stops.

The dog's plumed tail wags.

"What about him?" the wife says.

"He was asked to leave." The pastor's wife's face is a teakettle.

"What? Why?" But the wife has a feeling.

"Tilda Rainwater said something to him about his tattoo. She said his body is a sacred temple, you know. He laughed at her, held out his arm, and told her to go on and touch it if she wanted, it won't bite."

Not a surprise to the wife. She is embarrassed, though. She tried to suggest this morning it might be a bad idea to come, but the husband said as long as no one tried to convert him he'd be fine. Besides, he said, he loved Halloween. Now everyone will be talking about them, and her mother will be saying *what will people think?!* more than ever.

The wife is proud, too. Sometimes her husband says things she wishes she could say.

Back in the car on their way home, the husband brags to the wife. He describes Mrs. Rainwater's yellow teeth and fake smile. He tells how Mr. Rainwater nodded when Mrs. Rainwater said his body was a sacred temple.

"'Go ahead and touch it—it won't bite,'" the husband says. He laughs.

The wife says Mrs. Rainwater's hair, when she isn't wearing a Raggedy Ann wig, is a dyed, molded, and sculpted helmet, and she wears too much makeup, purple lipstick garishly wrong for her skin tone and teeth color.

The husband generates a scene in his mind for a novel he'll never write. He is the protagonist, Mrs. Rainwater the antagonist. His yellow-bellied sea snake tattoo comes alive and, in a glowing energy field, leaps off his wrist and grows and grows until it towers over Mrs. Rainwater.

Mrs. Rainwater screams and raises her arms.

The snake's tongue flickers.

It strikes, bites Mrs. Rainwater at the waist, shakes her, and swallows her bite by bite, her Raggedy Ann Mary Janes kicking, until she is a bulge swelling like a hernia under the snake's scales.

A storm breaks around the corner from their house.

"Lightning will strike you down," the wife says.

They both laugh.

The husband says, "Well, that sure was a waste of a good car wash."

At first the raindrops are fat like berries splatting on the windshield. Then a whiteout. The first red Barbie shoe hits a few seconds later, and the wipers flick it away. More Barbie shoes come down with the rain. They are red tracer rounds. The wipers flick them all away, but soon so many Barbie shoes are falling they make a dozen eraser-rub sounds when the wipers sweep them across the glass.

The tires *pock pock pock pock* over them. The steering wheel vibrates under his knuckles. The car hydroplanes a bit.

Soon, the shoes collect around the wiper linkages and slow the wipers down. The wipers jump over shoe clumps and smear red streaks.

Larger doll shoes, black Mary Janes, follow the Barbie shoes. They pound the roof and windshield and bounce off.

The husband is dumbfounded.

The wife appears to not notice anything out of the ordinary.

Tongue out, ears up, eyes darting, the dog watches it all from the wife's lap, enraptured.

SPEED LIMIT 55

ONE MORE TIME FOR DONNY DEADBORNE

For Zeke Jarvis

I'M A FEATURE COMEDIAN. THAT means I go on stage after the emcee opens the show with ten or fifteen minutes of announcements and lukewarm jokes. I'm on for about a half an hour, sometimes a little longer, right before the headliner, who carries the show with an hour-long set. Depending on the club, I do six shows a weekend, one on Thursday night, two on Friday night, and three on Saturday night. This weekend, I'll only do five. I started this seven years ago when I was twenty-three, and I've been featuring for four. I'm not sure I'll ever be good enough to headline, otherwise I'd probably be doing it by now. Most of the time, I'm okay with that.

My first time on stage was at the Safehouse, a Milwaukee spy bar with secret passageways and trick mirrors and a password required to get in. I was a tour guide at Miller Brewery then, misunderstanding people's questions if they asked them near the loud bottling lines. Reciting a memorized script for the tour groups and walking them down the same route over and over all day long soon made me feel like I was on a tape loop, dazed with boredom, so it wasn't long before I threw in deadpan one-liners about yeast and hops and kegs.

My brewery buddies dared me to sign up for the comedy open mic at the Safehouse. Tell a couple of your beer jokes from work, they all said. Of course I bombed. But it led to another spot the next week, and another, and so on, with a couple new jokes each time.

Eventually a round, greasy, drunk-off-his-ass booking guy offered me my first paid gig (twenty-five bucks and a free drink, maybe two if the manager liked me) at a bowling alley south of town. It took two years to polish and hone myself enough to move up from the steakhouses and Knights of Columbus halls to the comedy clubs full time, where, these days, I perform the same show at every venue, sometimes two or three times a night. There's an odd comfort in only doing material that's so familiar I could lip-synch my act. I've been tempted to try that, give my voice a rest once in a while. But I'd probably not hear the cue and end up horribly out of synch.

So, yeah, I'm deaf too. I lost a good part of my hearing when I was three. Fever. I'm not totally deaf, just hard of hearing enough to play it up and make a gimmick out of it. It makes me talk a little funny too—people often think I'm British. Road comics are a dime a dozen, and if you don't have a gimmick you ain't going nowhere. My opening line is *Heckling me is a waste of your time*, and the rest of my act is about misunderstanding everything I hear. Like when the telemarketer asks me if I'm interested in switching my long distance and I say *It's none of your fucking business how long my dick is.*

After my first round of one-liners, I say *Folks ask me all the time what it's like being hearing impaired.* The punch line is *Well, women take their underwear off when I tell them I read lips.* Of course that's a groaner, but I follow it with *And then they turn the lights off, and I have no idea what the hell they're trying to say.*

A LOT OF people say they would love a life on the road. These are the people who pretend to have read Kerouac and Nabokov. They'll tell you that Kerouac and Nabokov are their favorite authors. Sometimes I agree with these people. Nothing better than heading down the highway in the middle of the desert in New Mexico when the sun is just coming up, the corners of your windshield are still fogged, the taste of orange juice and toothpaste is still sour in your mouth, and your hair is still wet from your quick motel shower. Maybe Hank Williams or Judy Collins blaring on the stereo, and you've got nothing to worry about for another three hundred miles or so. Just you, Hank, and Judy. And a show at the end of the day.

But you do that every single day for a few years, and you can sing those songs better than Hank or Judy. You face nothing but three hundred miles of roadside signs that point out where everyone just like you has stopped for no reason other than to pick up a Milky Way and a local sights brochure. You'll admire the picture of a fancy resort on the cover, and you'll toss it in the backseat and never read it again.

Three hundred miles of passing semis, vast stretches of cactus and shrubs, high hills in the distance, the passenger seat empty the whole way, and all you want to do is stop in Las Cruces and find that Mexican restaurant you ate at when you were a kid dreaming of a life of travel. You remember that Mexican restaurant had a tree growing in the middle of it through the ceiling.

But you can't think like this, or you're not going to be in any mood to do your show.

Let me tell you how I got in the mood for tonight's show. About an hour out from town, I started playing "Silent Night" and "Jingle Bells" on my car horn. If you time it just right, it doesn't matter if the tune is a little off. Try it sometime. You get pissed at the guy in front of you, just give him a blast of "Grandma Got Run Over by a Reindeer."

After ten miles of caroling on my horn, the excitement wore off, so I wondered how long it would take to completely empty my windshield washer fluid reservoir. I ran the whippers —

By the way, I can't hear the difference between wipers and whippers. They sound almost the same to me, and they look almost the same reading lips. When I was young and first learned what windshield wipers were, I thought they were whippers. I know better now, but it's still fun to call them that.

Right?

Anyhow, I ran the windshield whippers and washer fluid

non-stop while tooting "Angels We Have Heard on High," and it took about six minutes for it to run dry. Never mind that the cars behind me were trying to run me off the road by this point. If you were out on Highway 41 this afternoon, and your car got splashed, yeah, that was me.

SPEED
LIMIT
55

ANY PERFORMER WHO tells you we aren't in this for love is lying. But being a comedian ain't like being in a rock band. Most of us only get miles and miles of yellow center lines pointing in a direction we've probably been down before. One or two lucky ones *will* be touched by someone's ten-foot pole.

Meanwhile, the rest of us shake hands, sign a soggy napkin or two, pose for a picture maybe, but if you're not super famous the customers only ask you to do these things if they think you've given them their money's worth. On Monday morning, they'll go to work and tell their colleagues about, say, this funny deaf guy they saw at the comedy club on Saturday night.

But they probably won't even remember your name. The only thing you've left behind is your fingerprints on the motel alarm clock's snooze button.

SPEED
LIMIT
55

IN THIS BUSINESS, it's either love or the road, never both.

The one woman I always came home to anyway, however, was Katelyn. With her, I discovered that sliced

Granny Smiths are finest soaked in dry red wine, which tasted best right off her lips. She loved how I kissed and kissed and kissed her until we were drunk. It's not that she didn't love me—it's just that I failed over and over again at making the choice.

I remember one morning when I was out on the road for a month. I left my motel, mailed her a post card, drove another couple hundred miles, went up on stage again, and had fun with a crowd of about two hundred and fifty people at a supper club in the middle of nowhere.

A young woman in the front row winked at me and looked me over several times. When I got off stage, I had the waitress send her a beer. The headliner commented on the young woman in the front row's expensive jewelry, but she only held the beer bottle up and heckled him.

After the show, I sat at the bar by the main doors and waited for her to come out from the show room. But she just high-tailed it right out of the place and into the parking lot without stopping to talk to me. The January moon reflected on her necklace, and she disappeared among all the cars and people.

Late that night, I was lying in bed in my motel room with the curtains open. Even with my hearing aids out, I could hear a truck approach on the highway. It must have been a mail truck because my post card to Katelyn was singing as it passed.

You think I'm kidding about that. That's what loneliness on the road does to you.

SPEED
LIMIT
55

SOMETIMES I WONDER why Katelyn stayed with me as long as she did. Maybe it was the quasi-glamorous lifestyle, the hobnobbing with comics she recognized from HBO and Comedy Central and *The Tonight Show*, the seediness of the whole thing. Or maybe she even felt a little sorry for me.

I was still a local emcee when we met, about to break into featuring. The microphone wasn't turned on when I opened the show at Donovan's Reef that night, and I didn't know it. I'd had one too many rum and cokes to drown the sore throat and headache creeping up on me, so I was nowhere close to the top of my game. I thought the people yelling that they couldn't hear me were hecklers. So I did the first few minutes of my set with the microphone turned off until the lanky owner came up on stage in a huff and turned it on for me.

Katelyn introduced herself after the show. She knocked over my hard lemonade, handed me a stack of napkins to wipe it up, bought me a buttery nipple, and took me to her house for a massage, some aspirin and tea, and a bubble bath.

Whatever it was that she saw in me, she eventually learned that there isn't all that much money to be made for an undiscovered feature act, even one who works the comedy clubs almost every weekend of the year and does one-nighters at resorts and private parties the rest of the week. No insurance. No benefits. My car has 236,428 miles on it, and it's only five years old.

SPEED LIMIT
55

IT'S BEEN A year since I was last here in upper Michigan at Keeper of the Fire Tropical Casino, but it feels like I've never left. They've put me in the same hotel room. I've somehow brought along the same stage clothes to wear as last time. Even the audience looks exactly the same. Regulars sit in the same chairs. The same drunk snowmobile mechanic from Escanaba stands up and pulls his pants down when I tell my cochlear implant joke. *I'll show you a cochlear implant*, he shouts. The same bouncer drags him out. The same friend from back home texts me after the show to see how it went. I can't get steaming hot water in my room, just like when I was last here. I spend ten minutes in the same tepid Jacuzzi. Same bath salts, same rough towel marked with a black C in the corner, same cigarette butt overlooked under the hotel services booklet. Before bed, the same Britney Spears special is on TV, same channel, same time.

SPEED LIMIT
55

ONE SUNDAY MORNING last July, on a weekend when I was working my home club for once, Katelyn sat up, tucked her long bed-head brown hair behind her ear, bit her lip, and looked under the covers By the way she shot out of bed and into the bathroom, I didn't have to ask what unexpectedly early problem she was having.

I pulled some pajama bottoms and a dirty T-shirt out of the hamper and drove down the block to the store. I picked up a box of tampons and started toward the registers. A stout woman in a pink sweatshirt and black leggings was pushing a cart loaded with diapers, ground chuck, Hamburger Helper, soda bottles, and frozen pizzas. She stopped me right there in the feminine care aisle while I was holding the tampons box to tell me she saw the show at Giggles Café last night and thought it was phenomenal.

Usually I don't mind running into people who recognize me. But I was in my pajamas and slippers, no jacket on. My hair was all wild, my stubble was itchy, and I was stinking like last night's whiskey sours, cigarettes, and sex, which, now that I look back on it, had been restrained and tentative, Katelyn quiet and rhythmic and far away, a stark contrast from her usual bucking and clawing.

I actually let the woman in the store take a picture of me with her phone. I almost told her to piss off, but I didn't know what else to do except be nice to her. I didn't want her to tell all her friends that she ran into the funny-deaf-guy comic at the store and he was acting like an asshole.

After I paid and was on my way back to Katelyn's house, I started writing a new bit in my head based on that experience, repeating it over and over to myself so I wouldn't forget it before I wrote it down. Something about how my girlfriend sent me to the store for some Kotex, and it busted up our relationship because I thought she told me to go get some ho sex.

Katelyn came out of the bathroom a few minutes after I delivered the box to her. She sat down next to me on the couch we'd bought together. She announced that her ex-boyfriend, the yacht company executive, had been coming around again—for quite some time now, in fact—while I was gone. He was taking her to Spain next week for the rest of the summer and fall, and she said it would be best if I was out of her house by the time she got back. She said she was sorry and started to cry, so I held her for a while, numbly wanting to ask details and yet not, feeling as if I knew them anyway.

SPEED
LIMIT
55

NOW IT'S THE second night of our five-show run at the casino. I spent the afternoon driving around the backwoods highways looking for something to do. I stopped in at the Chamber of Commerce in town to find out what some of the local sights were. The lady at the information desk suggested I might enjoy the comedy show at the casino.

"No shit?" I said to her.

I haven't worked with this weekend's headliner before. Her name is Smidgen. Women headliners are rare in this business. Midway through her act, Smidgen pulls a Hostess fruit pie from her bra. She tosses it to a heckler in the front row after he catcalls her. She pulls out a calendar and pen and asks the man when he's free for a date.

He says he's married.

"Is your wife here? No? Then let's have our date right now." She pulls a bottle of Heineken from her bra. "Don't like beer, huh?" So she pulls out a pine-colored bottle of champagne. The man pops the cork, and they each take a swig. She pulls a disposable camera from her bra. "A souvenir," she says and takes the man's picture.

There's just no other way to say it. She has big boobs.

Okay?

After the show, I ask her how she keeps all that stuff from falling out. "I'd love to show you sometime," she says.

The next night, it's ten below zero outside. She lugs in her paper bag full of props to the green room to get ready. She yelps when she tucks in the cold bottles.

When I get off the stage, she's waiting at the side. Before the emcee calls her name and she goes up, she places my hand on her breast. The beer bottle is hard and pointed through her blouse. She moves my hand to her other breast, where the champagne bottle is as heavy and bulky as a cowbell. The people sitting near us look at me like I'm some kind of pervert.

SPEED
LIMIT
55

LIKE SMIDGEN AND her boobs, sometimes I use my played-up deafness as a weapon. I don't always understand what a heckler is saying if I can't read his lips when he heckles me, so it's easy for me to tear him apart for picking on the poor handicapped comedian. One time, though, during an especially tough show at Hondo's Comedy Lounge, everyone was real restless and tipsy, and nobody was laughing much. I understood a big beefy guy with his wallet on a chain loud and clear.

"Suck my dick!" he said.

The crowd just went nuts when I put my hands on my hips and said, "Again?"

SPEED
LIMIT
55

A FEW YEARS ago, at The Twin Cities Skyline Club, a young man in a shirt and tie tried to impress his future mother-in-law. He slipped me a fifty slowly and obviously so that his future mother-in-law would see. I put it in my pocket. He shook my hand and went on to say how much fun they all had.

"Why aren't you in Vegas?" he said.

I think he also slipped the emcee a twenty. But he didn't ask the emcee why he wasn't in Vegas.

Next was a blond, dumpy woman in gilded glasses and loopy, beaded aquamarine necklaces.

"You're living my dream," she said after she took both my hands in hers. "And you have the funniest little accent. Where you from?"

"Deafmark," I said, and I immediately turned to shake the hand of the person next in line after her.

"Oh, that sounds like a nice place..."

The young man who tried to impress his mother-in-law came nudging his way back in the door and asked me to return his fifty bucks. Maybe I shouldn't have done this, but I smiled at him and pretended I couldn't hear him. When he asked again, I said, "Thank you for coming, glad you enjoyed the show, drive safe."

SPEED
LIMIT
55

ONCE IN A while, I philosophize that this profession is like knowing how far it is to the next town—you've traveled down the same highway so many times you don't notice the road signs anymore. Off stage, I sometimes hear my jokes in my sleep, but other times people at parties say *Hey, what's your best one-liner?* and I'm stumped and nothing comes out.

A full-time road comic is like a music box that just keeps cranking and cranking, and there's no life to the music because it just keeps turning and tinkling the same thing again and again, but I have to remember that somebody somewhere is still going to open the music box for the first time and be amazed.

SPEED
LIMIT
55

AN ELDERLY MAN in a John Deere cap, his white hair sticking out like little wings, approaches Smidgen, who is sitting at the corner of the bar near the back of the casino's comedy club in the shadows. The show is over. The last couple of lingerers from the crowd are filing out. Cigarette smoke swirls around the light bulbs, and the waitresses are already vacuuming the floor for the next show in an hour. Smidgen's broad back is to the approaching man in the John Deere cap. She apparently doesn't know the man is approaching until she feels him tap her shoulder.

"Hey," the man in the John Deere cap says. "I came to last night's show and loved it, and so I came to see you again tonight."

"Thank you," Smidgen says. She sips her beer and turns back around. She doesn't seem to want to talk to anyone.

"But I'm disappointed," the man in the cap says anyway. "You did all the same jokes. I want my money back because you did the same jokes I seen you do last night."

Smidgen ignores the man. "One more," she says to the bartender. She slides him her glass.

The man in the cap shakes his head and mutters something I can't hear as he walks out of the show room. Maybe the manager will give him a refund. I'll probably never see him again.

SPEED
LIMIT
55

I HAPPENED TO be in town a month after Katelyn got back from Spain. I agreed to meet her at Storybook Holler for the afternoon. Once again, like we used to, we would follow the Jack and the Beanstalk plywood pages all the way through to the giant's inevitable fall at the end. Katelyn had a surprise for me too, she'd written in her text message, just a small happy thing from Spain.

I arrived first and waited for her by the entrance, silently rehearsing reasons why I didn't bring a jacket on this cider October morning that came in all the way down to my ribs when I drank deep, why I was walking in sandals through the grass to the pumpkins.

Sometimes you can't let summer go, I said when she approached from the parking lot, her eyebrow raised. Because the hayride was closed the last time we came in the spring I also flapped our tickets like a grandson getting ready to show off a new card trick.

We walked together to the pumpkins without saying anything else. I turned one over, traced its ridges that were like rolling stairways, brushed off some dirt. I imagined we'd someday climb up a giant pumpkin stairway to places you only see in the background of others' travel snapshots, but at the far end of the orchard there was only a single bare Montmorency cherry tree wrapped in webs, and it reminded me of my grandfather's old hands pulling and stretching yarn in the light of the sun porch.

SPEED LIMIT
55

WHILE SMIDGEN IS on stage for the last show of the weekend at Keeper of the Fire, the emcee and I are at the bar watching the news on the muted, closed-captioned bigscreen TV. The reporter solemnly and silently announces that Mars is a graveyard for half the spacecraft ever sent there. The emcee is smashed by now. I've already forgotten his name. He asks me what I think of the scientists arguing that Mars is such an incredibly risky mission.

"It's not like they're shooting for the stars," he says.

The bartender is bored with us. I twirl my last two half-melted ice cubes. I fold up my chewed-on straw and leave it in my glass. Smidgen and her boobs have the crowd in stitches, but after seeing her act five times in three days I'm bored too. The drunk emcee follows me out to the parking lot for a breath of fresh air.

"Would you just look at that," he says.

Mars is the crown jewel city in a sky of millions of ordinary ones.

Mars should consider itself lucky that comedians haven't tried to go there. For now the only residents will be the broken and cold wreckage of probes that tried but never made it. And sooner or later our own home planet will be too littered with dream corpses floating in our aquarium atmosphere.

The drunk emcee and I stand in the parking lot and look up at the stars for a long time until I remind him that Smidgen is almost done. He staggers back in to close the show and thank the audience for coming.

What will happen to people like us? Will we go to Cape Canaveral and stow away on a rocket bound for the red planet because the odds are better that we'll make it there, because there's nowhere else for us to go?

SPEED
LIMIT
55

SOMETIMES I WORRY I'll end up like a bad parody of "The Night Before Christmas" that shows up every year in holiday form letters. I worry I'll be fifty-some years old, a little more deaf with age, maybe divorced because whoever came after Katelyn was dumb enough to say yes, living with my eighty-year-old mother, emceeing only amateur open mics at Mel's on Water Street because I'm too old and fucked up and worn out to be on the road full time. In spite of my years of experience and stage time, I'll probably drop the microphone when I pull it out of the stand. I'll mess up the name of the first comedian. I'll make fun of a heckler's ugly fat girlfriend. The heckler, already tanked so early in the night, will get up to punch me, but his ugly fat girlfriend will pull him back down in his chair and feed him some popcorn. I'll trip through a joke about Jeffrey Dahmer, failing to realize that in Milwaukee Jeffrey Dahmer jokes are never a good idea. I'll try to do impressions of Rich Little doing impressions of Ronald Reagan and Bugs Bunny singing "Take Me Out to the Ballgame." People will stumble-flee to the restrooms. The third comedian up will be a young, up-and-coming club professional who's passing through and has stopped in to try out some new material, but instead he will make me the butt of every joke.

In the back of my mind, I'll be more worried about how I'm going to pay some of the bills. I'll be worrying about my liver, by then turned inside out so many times by fast food and booze everyone will be amazed I'm still alive. I'll worry about lung cancer from all those years smoking unfiltered Camels to stay awake while alone in the middle of the night, driving home five hours to fall asleep in my own bed at the break of dawn rather than take one more night in a motel room. Maybe that's why I will forget the punch lines for the new jokes I'll have written.

The next morning, I'll give in to my mother and answer a Help Wanted ad for a delivery company that needs passengers to ride along so the drivers can use the carpool lane.

FOR NOW, AT least, I am still a driver. I'm heading back to Milwaukee for a few days off before my three-week swing through Illinois, Indiana, and Kentucky. A friend and his wife usually let me crash on the sofa in their basement now that I'm out of Katelyn's house. Can't afford a place of my own. Need to save for a down payment on a new car.

Before I left the casino, the emcee took my room because it has a Jacuzzi and his doesn't. I could tell from the way he and Smidgen looked at each other when I handed him my key card that they would be putting the Jacuzzi to good use.

The woods of upper Michigan are dark and cold. No moon. I watch for deer. It's a game that traveling performers play often, chicken with Bambi.

But the brown pine needle in the ashtray is one of my St. Christophers. I saved it from several hundred vacuumed from the trunk last December. Katelyn and I managed to string our Christmas tree with failed guesses snarled in the garland, creased wishes kinked in the tinsel. Both of us topped it with *Why don't you come with me* and *Why must you now leave* sad and unspoken behind the angel's eyes.

I also drive with a lighter from Spain, shaped like a flip flop. The flame appears from the toe. I might use *This smoke is made for walking* as a punch line. I'm rarely amazed at trinkets women bring me back from trips to Europe with other men, but sometimes I delude myself into thinking that my Dunhill Lights and my flaming shoe make me more sophisticated than my fellow performers in the green room. Stand-ups need their props while growing older on stages across America. The question is what will make us brittle first, the smoke or the road?

Two air fresheners swing from my mirror, scents long gone. One a red high-heeled shoe, the other a little blue shark. Home one night, I woke up because Katelyn wasn't in bed with me. I found her painting the kitchen. How lovely she was at one in the morning, whip-flip-flipping the paint roller up and down the walls, how superb the disorder of the stove pushed to the living room, the wine rack on top, bottles all around on the floor. The next morning, we went to the hardware store for wood trim and thinner, got distracted by the automotive aisle, where she opened the two air fresheners, put the shoe on the shark's head, and stood the shark upright so it teetered and fell over.

The green squirt gun in the cup holder is for protection, never mind that it leaks. Sometimes I pass through sleazy areas, hang out with tough characters. These days, after a show, I just want to crawl into bed with someone I love rather than the occasional wasted stranger. I took a break one weekend to help Katelyn pull up rotting shingles. In spite of shooting water at her from behind the chimney and allowing her, high up there on the roof, to push me down on my back to watch airplanes overhead, it was hinted my homecomings were numbered.

Even an umbrella is a St. Christopher. Mine always stays in the back seat, especially when it rains. Katelyn only came out on the road with me twice. One time, February in Tucson when it was wet, I froze, fear-caught and fascinated, in the rattler exhibit at the Desert Museum, umbrella closed and dripping, and she snuck up quiet from behind and wriggled her fingers up my back.

There's also a yellow ticket stub for the parking lot at Dollywood, left on the dashboard, faded from the sun. A car wash attendant tried to throw it away, but I stopped him. The second time Katelyn came with me, I was booked at a fundraiser near Gatlinburg to tell a couple jokes and sing "Viva Las Vegas" with thirty Elvis impersonators, the governor of Tennessee, and Dolly Parton. People cheered and sang along so loud I couldn't hear the band, so I kept time by watching Dolly and the governor's lips.

I don't often use the corkscrew under the armrest anymore. You never know where you'll need it, so it's convenient to have one handy. Katelyn and I run into each other every now and then at the Metro Market or Leon's Frozen Custard when I'm back in town. We'll go buy a bottle of Sangiovese to drink together slowly before leaving in our separate directions. She'll present me a harmless souvenir or two she's been keeping in her glove compartment. I won't ask her any questions. She used to have a tradition, while traveling herself, of writing post cards to me before anyone else. I'm sure she still does that, though she no longer sends them. They might be saved someplace I'll never see.

SPEED LIMIT 55

RHINESTONE HORSES

GRACE GARLAND HATED THE RHINESTONE rainbow bracelet her husband George had given her two days ago. It was cheap and tacky, she thought, and it snagged her nylons and made them run when she crossed her legs and rested her wrist on her knee, as she liked to do. But she wore it anyway because she often resigned herself to doing such things for him when he asked her to. Habit.

The empty casket rattled in the back of their spacious metallic green station wagon. The station wagon was almost twenty years old, and sometimes it killed at stop signs and wouldn't start again. And sometimes it overheated on the highway.

George was driving. Grace had never in all her life seen anyone so relaxed behind the wheel as George when he drove, and it irritated her. Everything George did irritated her. One of his bony hands was on top of the steering wheel, and his other hand rested on the headrest behind her. Her neck ached from leaning forward too long. She didn't want George's fingers touching her hair.

He hummed while he drove, and that annoyed Grace because the radio was turned off, but she held her tongue.

She remembered when, five or six years ago, she went in the cold garage one December evening and asked him if it was time to get rid of the wagon. No kids at home anymore, she'd said, so—since it was in such good condition—why not try and trade it in for something smaller. But George said no, wiped sawdust off his long chin, and continued sawing whatever it was he was sawing. As the electric blade droned and sawdust blew, he hollered that they'd never know when they'd need the wagon's cargo room. And besides, he added, it had a few years of life left in it.

It wasn't like George to give her presents. She examined the bracelet's cube-shaped rhinestones. They felt like rock salt and gleamed in the late afternoon sun that shone in her window and made her squint. She was too short for the visor to shadow her face. She turned the bracelet around and around on her wrist and wondered what made the stones change color as their angle shifted against the sunlight.

"You never told me where you got this bracelet," she said.

She was warm. The windows were rolled up, and the vents were closed, and this made the inside of the wagon smell sour and earthy. She wondered if George had left something under the seat. She took off her blazer and smoothed her blouse sleeves.

George turned his small head perched on top his long neck—Grace always wanted to knock that wobbly head off—and looked at her. His green eyes had a bored glaze as if he'd driven on that stretch of road twice a day every day for thirty years. He took his hand from behind her head and rubbed his short triangle nose that looked like a chip of flint. The skin of his face and nose had a brackish gray look.

At one time, he must have been magnificent, Grace thought. But she had to struggle to recollect, to see him, smell him, hear him, feel him as he once was. Yes, he had to have been different. Otherwise, she wouldn't have fallen in love with him and married him. But something blew into both their lives from somewhere like an acidic haze and distorted him into what he was now. No matter how hard she tried in that moment, she couldn't figure exactly when it was.

"If I wanted you to know where I got that bracelet," George said, "I would have told you."

"You got it on your trip, I'm sure," she said.

"Why do you care?"

"I just do."

She let the conversation trail off. Trying to talk to George lately, she thought, was about as hard as shaping a diamond with sandpaper. George had lots of it in his garage workshop, and he threw used sheets on the concrete floor when he was done with them instead of in the green trash can by the door.

The bracelet, though she thought it was probably the tackiest thing she'd ever gotten from anyone, reminded her of a pair of small rhinestone horses she'd had. The horses' colored rhinestones had been strung or clipped—she couldn't remember for sure, though she'd last seen them a few years ago—on wire, which was shaped to make legs, a body, a neck, and a head for each horse. Grace remembered both the horses had wire tails too, with blue rhinestones. Her mother bought the little horses—young Grace called them ponies—from the neighbors' rummage sale. She gave them to Grace because, she said solemnly, Grace needed to possess something pretty for once.

"Silence is golden," George said. "The glorious music of silence. Where can a man's thoughts go when he's lost in silence? Where can a man run when he's overtaken by running silence?"

"I'm not in the mood for your poetry," Grace said. Maybe she couldn't tell him the way his fingers brushed her hair when he rested his hand on her headrest drove her crazy, and maybe she couldn't tell him the way he drove rankled her, but she'd had enough of his recent attempts at poetry. His old habits might have settled into a dull loop she couldn't interrupt, an itch she couldn't scratch and just came to accept, but his recent ones were like a pin overlooked in a new shirt.

Poetry. The results of getting in touch with his inner self and his feelings, he'd announced one afternoon after getting back from one of his many trips to god-knows-where.

"What's wrong with my poetry?" he said.

"Every single day you shove a poem down my throat."

"I need to write poetry today," he said.

"Yes," Grace said, "planning your father's funeral has taken such an emotional toll on you."

"I need to get in touch with my emotions."

"You've said that before."

Grace thought it was disturbing how a man who could never express love or passion to her had turned to writing sappy love poems about inspiration from the angels that walked the earth. At first, she'd liked to think maybe he was trying to tell her something, something he'd come to realize was long overdue.

But Grace still hated the sweatpants and blue sweatshirt from the brewery he wore for the drive. They were too big for him, but George had always said to her that wearing bigger clothes made him look less puny than he really was. She couldn't remember when she'd stopped disagreeing with him about it.

"How come," Grace said, "you always have money for your trips?"

"What?"

Grace plowed on, "But a casket from the funeral home is too expensive? So we have to drive three hours to the wholesaler and three hours back?" Six hours of my life, she thought.

"It makes sense," George said, "to save some money on something we'll use only once."

"How can you say that? What about your father? He'll use it forever."

"No, we'll only use it once. One time." He gestured the number with his finger. "Once it's in the ground, it will have served its purpose. Out of sight, out of mind. You saw how much cheaper caskets are at the wholesaler warehouse."

"I deserve to know," she said, "where you're getting the money for this."

"From my father's insurance."

"I want to know where you're getting the money for your trips."

"Don't worry about it," he said.

"But I do," she said. "It's my money too."

"I've worked hard for that money," he said.

He started humming again.

"At least you didn't tell me to keep your eighty-four-year-old father in a refrigerator so you wouldn't have to pay more for rebooking and flying home early."

He continued humming.

Grace decide to give up talking to him for the rest of the day. She wondered again about those rhinestone horses she'd kept from childhood, wondered what George had ever done with them. When he went on his first trip away, which was right after his retirement party, she packed them in his suitcase with a note that said they would carry him safely on his journey. She also wrote that they would keep her in his thoughts since he wouldn't let her be there with him in person. Maybe it was silly, she thought, to have hoped the notes would change him when he came back.

Two weeks later when he came home, he didn't have the rhinestone horses. He had forgotten to pack them, he said, and must have left them at his hotel. He went in the kitchen with the ugly cabinets he'd built and made a quick phone call. A few minutes later, he came in the bedroom, where she was already in her nightgown and reading a magazine, and informed her the horses had not been found.

Those damn cabinets. Too white. They gave the kitchen a sterile look, and when the new fluorescent light flickered on the cobalt blue flour and sugar jars he'd bought and made everything look hazy and metallic, Grace swore she'd never be able to cook in there again. But she got used to it eventually. Every now and then, however, when she was in an especially irritable mood, the garish and washed-out whiteness of it all still hurt her eyes.

George stopped humming and started speaking.

"Boston," he said, staring out the windshield. His head tilted back so that his long chin jutted out, and he looked down his short brackish nose. "Boston, embrace me in the bosom of the salty Atlantic. How I yearn to return once more to your shores and your delicate lobsters, though I have felt your touch many times previous. Though I last visited you just two short days ago, why must I drive far from you now in my time of woe, my time of delirious sadness…"

So that's where he's been going, Grace thought. She'd never asked why he'd wanted to go away without her after his retirement, and she never argued with him about it either. She'd just wanted him to go. She looked forward to spending some time without him, some time putting in a couple extra hours at the flower shop or catching up with the neighbors or her old friends she'd lost track of as the kids grew up. And she looked forward to him coming back a new man, rejuvenated with energy only a trip can bring. But she only looked forward to that the first time. Now she searched for clues in her memory that would reveal how he had come to desire going to Boston in particular. Of all places. So often. Once would have been fine. Maybe twice. But not eight or nine times a year.

Grace was tired and had hoped to sleep on the long drive. But her husband had an annoying way of tapping the gas pedal with his foot and making the car surge forward every few seconds. Keeps it from overheating, he'd said a long time ago.

They were heading south on Highway 13. Grace turned

away from him and looked out the side window at the flat farms and the distant groves of maple trees rolling by. The leaves were lit with dazzling reds, oranges, and yellows. They passed a snowman made of enormous twine balls. Then a cemetery. Then a rusting robin-egg-blue Impala parked on top a farm silo.

Grace turned in her seat and craned her neck to see over the casket and out the station wagon's back window. She watched the Impala sedan on the silo disappear in the distance behind them. She wondered how it got up there and wished she could sit high on top something and look down on all the world below her.

"Look at that horse running there," she heard George say, "along the ditch a ways."

She faced forward again. The horse was up ahead a few hundred feet, trotting in the same direction they were traveling. It was honey brown, with a flowing mane, a bouncing tail, and rippling muscles under its tight skin. Its muzzle and forehead were white. It turned its head to the side as if listening to the car approach, but it continued trotting forward.

She leaned back in the seat and stared at the horse. Such a magnificent thing, she thought. Why was it running along the road by itself?

George drifted the car into the oncoming lane to give the horse room when they overtook it. But the horse stopped suddenly, turned, and stood so that its head and front legs were over the highway. Its ears flicked backward as weight shifted from one front leg to the other.

All four legs sprang forward with energy like snapped

steel cables, and the horse sprinted directly in front of them in a mad dash to cross the road.

"Sit tight," George said.

Suddenly the garish white cabinets and flickering fluorescent light—why didn't he just take the damn thing back and get another one that didn't flicker?—danced in front of the car, erased the dashboard, the windshield, the horse, the trees, the road, everything, and they were coming closer and closer too fast to avoid. A zing of alarm whipped from her head to her toes—cavities, Grace thought, I have cavities again, like when I ate a handful of chocolate-covered cherries all stuffed in at once, and my whole mouth just went *zing zing zing*, and the nerves under my cheekbones tingled for an hour—and Grace pressed both feet hard on the floor and grabbed the armrest on the door to brace herself for the crack and splintering of the smooth and painted wood, the shattering of the cobalt blue jars, the raining down of sparks and shards of glass from the fluorescent light.

The kitchen disappeared, and the world roared back.

A moment before impact, the horse bolted off course from crossing the road. Instead, it shot in the same direction George and Grace were driving, as if attempting to outrun them.

But they hit it. Highway speed. As far as Grace could tell, George never braked. In that awful second, she wanted to close her eyes, but she watched, half dismayed and half fascinated, as the horse's hind legs collapsed over the hood and its front legs flared up in the air. Its hind end came down hard on the hood too—a horrible, hollow thudding and crumpling sound. The horse toppled to the left and rolled off the station wagon.

Finally, the severe squeal of brakes. A burst of smoke covered the windshield. The casket rattled forward and knocked into the back of Grace's seat. The grating of the brakes was long and loud. The station wagon lurched to a stop directly in the middle of the oncoming lane. The smell of burnt rubber and oil filled the air, and a hissing sound came from somewhere near the front of the car. Thin smoke from under the hood curled and twisted over the windshield.

Grace and George sat in silence for a few seconds. She still gripped the armrest, and her feet still pushed into the floor as if stomping on an imaginary brake pedal. George took his hands off the steering wheel and rubbed Grace's shoulder.

"Now, now," he said. "I'm all right."

Grace looked at him and thought only that he'd just killed a goddamn horse. Did he just kill a goddamn horse? She opened her door and stepped out onto the highway. The autumn chill was a welcome relief from the station wagon's stuffiness. The air smelled like roasting pine nuts.

A lawn ornament business was across the road from where they'd come to a stop. Curious and mortified-looking shoppers-turned-onlookers milled around parked cars and displays of little windmills, lawn balls on pedestals, and fake deer. Grace imagined it must have been quite a sight for the people to see, an old rattling station wagon crashing into a horse and roaring to a stop right in front of them.

The horse was on its side about two hundred feet back, its front legs bucking and clawing, its back legs twisted and limp. It raised its head and lunged its neck forward each time it attempted to stand on its front legs. It made a grunting and rumbling sound as if trying to clear something clogging its throat.

Grace covered her mouth. She couldn't believe the pain and fear, even from that distance, in the animal's dark eyes. The eyes bulged from their sockets. The nostrils flared with each terrified huff of air.

And when she looked away — it was as if her eyes stopped working and she saw nothing, focused on nothing — she wondered if George might have — just might have — hit it on purpose. Something to write poetry about. Couldn't he have braked sooner? Couldn't he have swerved?

George's door slammed shut, and his sneakers squeaked on the pavement. As Grace breathed in and out to slow her racing heart, her vision came back slowly like water bleeding through a paper towel. George came around the front of the car, stopped with his hands on his hips, his head wobbling on his neck, and studied the smashed front end.

"The car's still running," he said. "I think I can drive it up the road to Pittsville, long as I hurry up and change this flat here in front and don't shut the motor off. I think oil is leaking out somewhere, so we got to get moving."

"Have it towed," Grace said quietly. She kept her hand over her mouth and her eyes away from the horse. But she couldn't, no matter how hard she tried, keep from looking at that horse again. In some strange way, she thought, looking at the horse was easier than looking at George.

The horse didn't buck its legs as furiously now but scrambled them around on the crushed red granite shoulder of the road. Grace supposed it was more an effort to distract itself from its pain rather than stand up.

"Didn't you hear me?" George said once more. "You have to help me pull the casket out so we can get the spare tire."

She wanted to go to the animal, but she didn't want to watch it suffer either. She wanted to offer it comfort, take away its pain somehow, but she was sure it wouldn't let her get close enough.

She turned back toward the car, feeling guilty for leaving the horse alone, feeling too, through her shoes, the crunch of granite pebbles on the pavement. She couldn't look George in the eye. She didn't want to look at him at all. She blocked out the hissing and spitting of the motor, the whine of an approaching semi, the *Need some help?* offers from the onlookers at the lawn ornament business, some of whom were now milling around the damaged station wagon.

George opened the station wagon's back gate and, with the help of one of the men standing around, pulled the simple, unadorned casket out and let it clatter and boom onto the side of the highway. Grace thought he dropped it as carelessly as a baby pushing its bowl off its highchair. George crawled into the back of the car, his sneakered feet hanging over the bumper, as another one of the men kneeled and set to work whirling the jack handle around and around.

Grace thought it was too chilly outside and wished for her blazer in the station wagon. But she never wanted to go in it again. A new wind gusted and swung the station wagon's back gate shut on George's feet. He kicked the door open, and a howl of frustration mixed with the chattering of the women and children who stood around Grace now. A boy in a black baseball cap ran up the road to the horse and kicked it in the ribs before running back and standing behind his mother's legs. Grace turned away from him.

"The police are coming," she heard someone yell.

George crawled feet first out of the car, swearing and pulling the spare tire. He stood up, bounced the tire on the pavement, and rolled it around to the front. One of the men already had the damaged wheel off.

She wished the jack would collapse and send the car crushing George. She folded her arms around herself and heard only the horse's snorting and huffing behind her. She was surprised it didn't whinny or scream. She didn't know for sure if a horse could scream but imagined it should do something other than snort and wave its legs around after getting hit by a car.

"It's one of Frickenstein's," an old man in dirty overalls said. "At least it looks like one of Frickenstein's. Just the other day I says to Frickenstein, 'Frickenstein,' I says, 'you better pen them up better...'"

Grace didn't pay attention. The approaching semi had slowed and now maneuvered around the disabled station wagon. It blasted its horn twice and continued on its way.

From somewhere far down the road toward the south came the hum and chirp of a siren. It grew louder, and soon the red and blue lights sparkled where the road seemed to meet a grove of trees. It only took a minute for the police cruiser to coast to a stop at the scene. Grace left the group of women and children and walked up to join the deputy as he was getting out.

He was a short and fat young man, about twenty-five years old, Grace guessed. His buttons strained and his fleshy white neck bulged over his buttoned collar. His black eyes were quick and shifty, and his shaved head shone in the afternoon sun.

"Everyone all right?" he said.

"Can you please do something about the horse?" Grace said.

"Let me see if everyone's okay at the car first. Everyone okay?" He strode over with long, purposeful strides, his boot heels clicking, his round chest stuck out and his bulging stomach sucked in. George and the other men ignored him. George heaved the spare tire in place, settled it, and reached for a lug nut on the ground.

Grace followed the officer and tugged on his fleshy arm. "Everyone's fine," she said. "No one's hurt. But the horse is—"

The officer turned to her. "Is the horse dead?"

"Not yet. It's hurt."

"Let's take a look."

Grace followed his clicking heels again, steeled herself to look at the horse up close for the first time, and avoided meeting its eyes. Its front legs quivered. Its broken back legs were in disfigured heaps.

"Holy Jesus," the officer said. "You hit him hard, I see."

"Do you know who he belongs to?" Grace said.

"Can't say I know too many horses around here."

Grace looked at his gleaming name tag. Deputy Goldsmith.

"Maybe his owner can come and kill it," she said. "I think I heard someone say it belonged to a Frickenstein."

Goldsmith whistled. "Can't say I know a Frickenstein

either. I'll do some investigating…"

And Grace caught something flicker over his face, a quick little wave of uncertainty and indecision, like a ripple in a sheet of paper. Goldsmith put one hand on his waist, squinted, and with the other hand unsnapped his holster.

"I hate to do this without investigating, but that poor things needs to be—"

"Can I do it?" Grace said, interrupting Deputy Goldsmith.

"Beg pardon?"

"Can I shoot it?"

"What?"

"Please give me your gun."

"Well, I—"

"Are you going to give it to me or not?"

Grace looked back to the station wagon. George stood up among the few men kneeling around him and turned toward her, his long neck craning. He wiped his hands on his sweatpants and started walking to her. A grease smear ran down the left side of his face. The grease was the same color as his thinning hair, which blew up off his head. His brewery sweatshirt was torn. His mouth moved. He was saying something, but Grace was too far away to hear. She was sure it must have been a couple lines of poetry.

Behind George, a little windmill turned. A wind chime clinkled. The sun shimmered on a red glass ball on a gold pedestal. The casket sat silent under the clear sky.

Grace knew then he'd never made that phone call to the hotel where he claimed to have forgotten her rhinestone horses. He'd pretended. Carried on a conversation with the dial tone. She felt stupid for never having checked the phone bill.

When she grabbed the gun, the deputy's shifty black eyes went wide. He gasped, and his sucked-in stomach fell down over his belt as if it were a sack of cornmeal flopped over the edge of the countertop. The gun was light in Grace's hand — an empty plastic toy. A rhinestone horse. And of course the trigger didn't pull back — it was stuck.

She was in her kitchen again, surrounded on all sides by white cabinets reaching up higher than she could see, white countertops around her boxing her in so she couldn't get out, cobalt jars everywhere. On top of the refrigerator, on the stove burners, even in a huge gleaming kettle of boiling water, on the floor around her feet, stacked in towers that came to her waist, and when the towers of cobalt jars grew into prison bars the rhinestone horse floated from her hand, turned its head one way and then the other as if looking for its mate, and stared her in the eyes, flared its little rhinestone nostrils that glittered in the flickering fluorescent light (*damn it anyway, why didn't he just go get another one that didn't flicker?*), swung its tail, and stamped its foot on the empty air it floated in.

The gunshot collapsed everything — the towers of jars, the white cabinets, the floating rhinestone horse — in a swirling whirl of dust. The horse's neck and front legs went slack on the ground.

Deputy Goldsmith stood next to her, both of his hands clutching the gun, still smoking and still aimed at the horse (*when did he take it from me? or did I just give it back to him? how did he shoot it if the trigger was stuck?*). His eyes were closed, and his stomach heaved like, Grace thought, a man's stomach will when he's trying not to cry but can't help it.

George had stopped between the car and Grace. His hands covered his eyes. His lips quivered. His sweatpants looked as if they'd fall off him. The casket behind him reminded Grace of a picture she once saw in the paper of a derailed freight car.

She should have questioned George's trips, should have focused a little harder on finding out where he went so much and why, should have refused to accept the trips from the beginning. George's sentimental, stupid poems had been trying to tell her something, all right.

To start what would from now on be a long chain of refusals, Grace unclasped her rhinestone rainbow bracelet and let it fall on the highway next to the horse.

SPEED LIMIT
55

FOOLS OF NATURE

GLENDA WASN'T LOOKING FORWARD TO spending all night alone in her bus in a January Wisconsin blizzard. She drove north on the four lane in the middle of dark dairy country not really knowing where she was. The snow blew everywhere—up her motor coach's huge windshield, up in white dust devils over the highway signs, and over the road so that the road disappeared and reappeared again a few seconds later. The center line was gone, had been gone for an hour, but every now and then patches of black, iced-over pavement that looked like giant footprints appeared through the snow.

Her CB radio sputtered and whooped, and once in a while only a garbled voice cut in. The wind and snow were driving away even the radio, and Glenda ached at the prospect of losing the warmth of those canned voices that burst through the chilly air of the empty bus.

She'd forgotten her charging cable. On the console next to her lunch tote and empty thermos, her phone was dead.

All the lights in the bus were off. The rearview mirror

reflected only the first five rows behind her. After those, the rest disappeared in the dark. The defrosters weren't working. Her mirror was fogged up, and so were most of the windows on the bus. She wiped the windshield with her sleeve and made a small hole just big enough to see out. The rest of the windshield, as large as a blackboard, stayed fogged up.

Glenda had turned off the heat. She was tired, as any sixty-year-old would be at the end of a long day driving, and she hoped that a chill would help keep her awake through the storm. There were warm gas stations and truck stops out there in the cold. Somewhere. She pictured them buried in the snow as if they were pencil boxes. But she couldn't remember it having snowed *that* much in a long time.

Maybe the global warming is real, she thought.

Snow caked the letters on the big green highway signs. Her icy headlights didn't illuminate them anyway. She couldn't read the smaller blue signs either, the ones which could tell her where to find some relief and a snack. She thought about stopping and brushing some snow off one of those signs, but they were too tall. She hadn't brought any boots either.

She drove on, thinking if only those people talking about global warming really were right, praying they might be, praying that all of a sudden the atmosphere would cloud over like Venus, and the sun's invisible stingers would inject themselves into Earth and fry away all the snow caked on the highway signs so she could find her way home.

If she kept following the pavement footprints in the snow, she would get there.

Eventually.

She sighed and tightened her grip on the steering wheel. She wished she had a bigger coach, one of the fancy ones that wouldn't skid on ice and snow even if she were driving ninety. Surely they made coaches like that, she thought. If science could create global warming, why couldn't it build a bus that wouldn't skid on ice and snow even if she were driving ninety?

The group she'd driven down to O'Hare was a small group of about twenty people. Her company didn't need to send out the smaller coach very often, but, on Glenda's assignment the day of the January blizzard, they had.

She passed a pickup truck stranded on the shoulder. Its hazard lights winked at her. Orange and red mushrooms bloomed across her foggy windshield and shrank away as if they'd been sucked up by a vacuum cleaner.

The truck disappeared into the darkness behind her, and a car's lights ahead peeked from the flying snow. This vehicle was down in the ditch to the left. The car's front end was buried in a drift, and the back end was sticking out. It was a newer car, a luxury car, one with a huge back end, a fake tire well on the trunk.

For the first time in a few hours, Glenda smiled. A garbled voice sliced the cold air inside the bus. Glenda felt a little better. She had no idea what the unseen fellow was saying, but he made her feel a little more relaxed, made her think that staying out all night in the snow was perhaps a little more bearable.

She felt her husband with her in the cold bus, in the cold emptiness. She listened to the windshield wipers squeak and the tires crunch. She was going only about twenty miles an hour, so the engine growled faintly from the back.

Near the door, down in the footwell, a seat was folded up against the windshield. An over-enthusiastic tour guide sometimes sat there, but now it was empty like the thirty other seats on the bus. Her husband wanted to sit there, but she figured he could just sit in the row behind her. She wasn't going to pull over just to fold out the jump seat.

Nice weather today, Frank, she thought.

There was no answer. He never answered her when he knew he'd been proven right.

You were right. I should've told them I was sick today, she continued.

Still no answer. She waited a few minutes.

Say something, she thought.

He could be so proud sometimes. Stubborn too. She focused her attention back to the road. If he was going to ignore her, then she was going to ignore him.

After a few minutes, her thoughts wandered again. The high school group she'd driven down to O'Hare was going to Paris. Their teacher had sat in the tour guide seat the whole way down and told Glenda all about it. Glenda listened politely, but she'd heard it all before. French club. New London High School. Raised money selling candy bars. Students worked so hard. So proud of themselves. Blah blah blah.

Paris in January, Glenda thought. What's it like?

Cold, her husband answered. Damp.

She ignored him.

She wondered if their plane had taken off or if it was

sitting on the runway in the snow. In the cold darkness.

Once, she'd flown back from her daughter's wedding in Tucson. It was the middle of March. Warm in Tucson — cold in Wisconsin. She'd changed planes in Minneapolis. After boarding and taxiing out to the runway, the plane with Glenda in it sat there for five hours in a blizzard — from eleven at night until four in the morning — before it finally took off. All the lights in the plane were turned off, and when the de-icing trucks came their headlights scared her. She felt as if she were buried in a deep shipwreck, and when the de-icing trucks pulled away into the black blizzard so the plane could take off she thought they looked like submarines leaving the wreck to surface.

She'd felt that way when her daughter moved to Tucson too. Her daughter was a submarine leaving her in the silence of the deep.

The cold air, seeping up through the floor of the bus, nibbled Glenda's toes. She flexed her feet. The bus slowed down as her right foot came up off the gas pedal, but she pushed it back down again when some warmth crept back into her toes.

The darkness outside had not changed.

It was only early evening. Four hours ago, she dropped the group off, but to Glenda it felt like four days. It was still light out in Chicago when she left. She just got through rush hour traffic in Milwaukee when the storm started. It would take her about five or six more hours, she estimated, to get back to New London in the winter weather. She would drop the bus off downtown, start her car, and be home fifteen minutes after that.

Maybe the dispatcher tried to call her on the dead phone with instructions to find a motel and bring the bus back after the storm. Maybe the dispatcher was one of the woobling voices on the CB radio she couldn't understand.

Frank was right—she was vain. She feared people would make fun of a hearing aid, so she didn't get one. Frank was right that her vanity got the best of her.

But it wasn't so much people making fun of her as it was admitting she was getting older. Age was a funny thing to Glenda. She didn't understand why, if the body regenerated new cells, people got old. How could people get old with all those new cells? If all those new cells completely remade the skin every couple weeks, why did skin wrinkle and sag? If all those new cells completely remade a new skeleton every ten years, why did bones start creaking and grinding?

Glenda probably should have pulled off the road for a motel room before she left Milwaukee, but, now that she was halfway home anyway, pushing on was the best course. Rooms were probably booked up by now.

An hour went by.

Another hour. She drove past car after car, all stranded on the side of the highway or in the ditch. After a while, a band of lights shone through the snow to her right, and she figured it came from a large building, maybe a factory. A few minutes later, the lights disappeared behind her.

Glenda was late for her nightly card game with Marlene, her neighbor. Glenda needed to see a friendly face. She didn't look forward to going home to an empty house. As much as she didn't look forward to going home to an empty house, a cold motel room wasn't any better, so Glenda was confident she'd made the right decision to keep driving.

She'd go to Marlene's, and Marlene would get out the worn deck of cards they always played with, slap it down on the table, and roar that hearty laugh that always made Glenda feel better.

How's Marlene, Frank said.

Not too bad, Glenda answered.

Give her my regards.

I will.

Marlene once told all her friends that Glenda had the prettiest name she'd ever heard. She said it made her think of meadows and pastures, sheep standing around quietly, wells pumping, and wheelbarrows squeaking along the ground.

Glenda smiled again. She thought her name was too ordinary. Nobody understands where Marlene gets those ideas, she thought, but everybody likes her anyway.

She wished she could call Marlene, but her phone was dead. She'd never figured out how to work everything on it, but her company had urged her to have one in case of an accident. People booked motel rooms on phones now without making a call and talking to someone.

If science could do that, why couldn't regenerated bodies stay the same age?

Like the storm, a warm tightness of having to powder her nose came from nowhere. She flexed her legs and arched her back. It didn't help much, but Glenda struggled to ignore her discomfort anyway.

You should have gone before you left, Frank said.

She wanted to tell Frank to shut up, but she didn't dare.

She hoped he wouldn't read her thought. It was funny, she knew. Sometimes she longed to hear his voice, but sometimes she cringed whenever he said something.

I should be in Tucson right now, Frank said.

We can't go to Tucson.

We should.

No.

She hated it when he brought this up. Her husband had loved going to Tucson to see their daughter. He claimed the weather cured his asthma. Glenda never understood how, all that dust flying around. But she had gone to their daughter's wedding alone.

You left me home, Frank said.

You were sick.

I could have traveled.

Staying home was the best thing for you.

Leaving me home was the best thing?

Yes, dear.

Bah.

She drove on. Another three or four hours, she estimated, and she'd be home. Marlene was probably waiting up for her. Maybe she was sitting at the table with the cards already out and a bowl of chips and salsa and guacamole too. Marlene made the best guacamole. Her secret was lemon juice instead of lime juice.

What about all the times you left me alone, she said to Frank.

I never left you alone.

Yes, you did.

Bah.

Stop saying that.

Bah.

Glenda hated his *bah*. It was his way of winning an argument, which, when she thought about it, really meant he had no other way of winning it. He got madder when somebody argued with him. She'd always thought to herself it would kill him someday. It did, when he got in an argument with his own body he knew he couldn't win.

You left me alone when you went hunting, she said.

Men are supposed to go hunting.

No, they're not.

Frank didn't say anything.

After a minute or two:

Bah.

The wipers squeaked and the tires crunched. Glenda sped up a little bit, and the growl from the back got a little louder.

Be careful, he said.

Yeah.

You'll crash.

In the last few weeks before his death, she took the job driving buses. She needed to get out of the house. It wasn't about money. He was making her crazy.

Bah.

She closed her mind off to him. He was still sitting behind her, but as long as she didn't acknowledge him he couldn't get to her.

She kept driving and driving.

After about another hour, she came to a long bridge. A car came up behind her in the left lane, went into a skid after it passed her, and crossed into the right lane directly in front of Glenda's bus. She tapped the brake pedal but then lifted her foot off.

Bad idea, she thought.

The car slowed down some, its brake lights flashing on and then off as first it skidded to the right and then to the left. It went off toward the shoulder, and the corner of Glenda's bus clipped the back bumper. The car spun in a snow cloud and went down the ditch directly in front of the expansion joint between the road and the bridge.

She thought of stopping to see if the driver was okay. He probably was. He hadn't been going all that fast, Glenda thought. There wouldn't be much damage to her bus either.

She kept going.

She'd tell the young guys in the head office back at the station that a deer had run out in front of her. The driver in the ditch could tell the police anything he wanted. They'd think he was just making up a story to cover the fact he'd been driving a little faster than he should have.

The wheels made a clanking sound as the bus crawled onto the bridge. The bridge went over a lake so the snow blew even more viciously.

Lake Butte des Morts, about an hour from home under normal conditions.

Glenda was surprised to be at the bridge already. She hadn't even seen the lights of Oshkosh. She slowed down a little and wiped the windshield with her sleeve. She peered ahead through the dark, straining.

The bridge went straight forward into the snow. About twenty feet in front of the bus, there was nothing but blackness. A tunnel of white blew on all sides of Glenda's vision — straight ahead, from the sides, from above, and from below — but she saw absolutely nothing beyond twenty feet.

She leaned back in her seat and slowed the bus down some more. She didn't want to hit the railing, and she briefly pictured her bus plunging straight down off the bridge and smashing through the ice into the dark water below. She relaxed her grip on the wheel and concentrated on keeping the bus going straight. She knew her tension might increase the chances of an accident.

Why couldn't science…?

It was a long bridge, about half a mile, but Glenda kept the bus at a crawling pace. A few minutes until back on land again.

In the summer, the bridge crossed sparkling blue water that crawled with water-skiers and fishing boats. She remembered a few times when the family had come to fish. She'd never enjoyed fishing, but it was one of the only things she could do with Frank. It was more enjoyable than going hunting with him. He never let her try hunting anyway.

"It's a man's sport," he always said.

But she went fishing a few times, mainly to keep him from griping about how she never did anything with him.

Of course she'd needed him when her sister died. It was early one late November morning when she got the call from the hospital. Frank was in the kitchen fixing some sandwiches to take hunting. After she hung up the phone in the bedroom, she let out a single sob and went to the kitchen with her hand over her mouth. She walked slowly across the cold linoleum floor in her bare feet and put her other hand on Frank's back. He never asked what was the matter. He threw the sandwiches in his cooler, snapped it shut, and walked out the door.

The frosty air that dashed in as the door swung shut made her nightgown ripple around her. She stood there a long time with her hand over her mouth, staring at where Frank had been. She watched the rosy dawn slowly emerge through the small round window in the center of the door.

She got dressed and asked Marlene to take her to the hospital.

Glenda imagined the sun was shining on the bridge once more. Water-skiers shouting and boats buzzing. She remembered what it was like to be in a small fishing boat down on the water, and she felt the up and down motion of the gentle summertime waves. Her face was warm in the light, and her hair was free in the breeze.

But the bridge was treacherous in the winter. It stretched so far over the ice, and the lake was so big.

Each year there were stories in the paper of deadly accidents. A wealthy executive on a business trip from Florida whips past a semi in his big Lincoln rental and fishtails on a patch of dark ice. Skids right under the trailer and crushes the roof of the car. A teenager shows off his new pickup to his girl. Pickup meets a heavy blast of icy wind carrying a wall of blinding snow. Hits the guardrail, bounces off of it, hits the rail on the other side, and flips over it. Boy and girl plunge into the dead water.

Glenda more and more uncomfortably had to go to the loo. She recalled an exit right beyond the bridge with a few gas stations, so she planned to stop there. She had not seen any exits for several miles now. Miles and miles. She didn't know if that was because of the weather or because she was too concerned with looking straight ahead, but she made up her mind to keep an eye on the right side of the road for the next exit sign.

It occurred to her that maybe snow storms like this one were mythical and powerful enough to erase exits, to pull them up into the clouds, or, most likely, to extend and stretch and pull apart space between roadways and exits so that gaps between snowflakes were entire other universes and exits were lost across vast universes and universes of snowflakes.

The storm certainly made her feel much smaller in a much larger universe.

Two sets of red lights came through the black curtain before the bus. At first, Glenda thought those two cars were traveling more slowly than her bus, but she realized they were completely stopped.

The bus slid a little to the right and to the left, but she kept her foot on the brake pedal. The wheels locked, and the bus continued sliding forward, the brake pedal pulsing like reflexes. She felt a tire catch a bare pavement patch, and the bus jerked and shuddered. Another tire caught a bare pavement patch and made the bus jerk again.

In a burst of snow sliding down from the roof and past the windshield, the bus stopped.

Glenda wiped the windshield with her sleeve once more, making a bigger hole this time. The two cars were directly in front of her. She looked down on them from her seat. Their brake lights still shone brightly, and they bathed her bus in a red glow.

She unclipped her seatbelt, opened the door, and stepped into the wind and the blowing snow. Ice pellets and small, sand-like snowflakes pelted her face and caught in her hair. She gasped at how bitter it felt outside and zipped up her coat. It was colder than she'd thought.

She went to the passenger window of one of the cars. The window rolled down, and a young woman's face emerged from the darkness inside. The woman was wearing a ski cap.

Glenda bent down so her face was close to the woman's.

"What's wrong?" Glenda said.

The car's driver was hidden in shadows, but the dashboard's soft green lights lit the passenger woman's face enough to look like a *Phantom of the Opera* mask. The woman's eyes were hidden in the darkness too, and Glenda shivered in the cold and wondered if she'd perhaps done the wrong thing by leaving the safety of her bus.

"Deer," the woman said. She nodded at her windshield.

Glenda straightened and looked in the direction the woman had indicated. She shielded her eyes and squinted.

Two deer stood about twenty feet in front of the cars. The headlights illuminated them in the snow, and Glenda wondered why she hadn't seen them. Every few seconds, a puff of snow clouded the deer and made them look like blurry paintings on a Christmas card.

They stayed right in the middle of the bridge, their heads up. They darted their heads around, first in one direction, then in another. They both pranced in a small circle and stood still again.

"We've been sitting here five minutes," the woman said, "but they won't get out of the way."

Glenda leaned in closer to hear, never taking her eyes from the deer.

"My husband tried inching up to them," the woman continued, "but they still wouldn't get out of the way."

"They don't know where to go," a deep voice said.

Glenda assumed the voice came from the husband behind the wheel.

The woman snapped at her husband, "You're just scared of hitting them and wrecking your new car."

"Damn right I'm scared of hitting them and wrecking my new car" he said. "Fifty-nine payments left."

"Jesus Christ," the woman said.

"They went to the side railing on the right," the man said, "like they wanted to jump out of the way. They stopped and went over to the other railing. They stopped there too."

At least that's what Glenda thought he said. It was hard for her to understand people talking in the dark under background noise like engines and wind and spiraling, howling universes between snowflakes.

Glenda pointed toward the opposite end of the long bridge. "Why don't they just turn around and go back that way?"

"They must not have thought of that," the woman said.

"I can't tell you when I ever saw deer so confused," the husband said. "Skittish things you'll ever see. Lord knows. They haven't tried jumping off the bridge."

"For crying out loud," Glenda said.

"Pardon?" the woman said. She leaned a little bit out her window and brought her head closer to Glenda.

Glenda ignored her and stared at the deer. They were

pretty in the snow, Glenda thought. They pranced gracefully, and the headlights emphasized every detail on their bodies—their fur's brown and gold hues, the moisture on their noses. A puff of snow blurred the deer again.

Glenda didn't know what to do. She needed to go to the bathroom, badly. She wanted to get home. She wanted to play cards with Marlene. She was so hungry she could taste the chips and salsa and guacamole she hoped Marlene would have waiting for her. The secret was the lemon juice.

The deer didn't look to her like they were going to move anytime soon, just sit on the bridge all night making up their minds which way they wanted to go.

Bring me my gun, she heard her dead husband say somewhere from the wind.

She hoped the deer heard him from somewhere in the wind too and would jump over the guard rail. Wishful thinking, she knew, but conjuring in her mind a danger to the deer could make it so.

She didn't have a gun. Even if she had Frank's, she wouldn't touch it.

But she thought maybe firing a shot in her mind would be more effective than Frank telling her to get his gun. Maybe a shot would scare them and make them jump. They would fall down off the bridge and crash onto the ice below, their legs flailing in all directions. They would bounce up and dash off into the night. The fall wouldn't hurt them, would it?

"I don't know what their problem is," the woman said.

Glenda echoed the husband in the car. "They don't know where to go," she said.

The man behind the wheel said something. A row of cars had lined up behind the bus and were honking their horns. She would have asked the man to repeat himself, but she was too busy being held up by the deer, too busy figuring this all out.

Frank told her to walk in front of the two cars blocking the bridge and stand in the yellow headlight beams throwing snow shadows. She did. He explained to her how to mentally measure the gap between the two cars. She did. She studied the front of her bus. She walked around again to the woman.

"Sit tight," Glenda told her.

"What?"

Frank guided Glenda by the elbow tramping through the blowing snow toward her bus. Snow pinched coldly in her shoes, wrapped its icy fingers around her ankles. She got in the driver's seat, and Frank instructed her to put the bus in reverse, as if he were a driving instructor. She backed up a bit, being careful not to bump the car behind her.

Careful of the car behind you, he said.

She swung the giant steering wheel all the way over to the left, like he told her. She drove the bus forward slowly and straightened the wheel again. She guided the bus between the two parked cars. She shifted her eyes from wing mirror to windshield to other wing mirror. Wing mirror to windshield to other wing mirror.

She'd make it. Just enough room.

But she scraped the door mirror of the car with fifty-nine payments left.

Watch out there, Frank said.

She didn't care. She was surprised he didn't swear at her,

but she still didn't care.

Frank told her to stop the bus and honk the horn one more time. The deer stood in her headlights, looking off to the side as if unaware of all the cars backed up now and the bus. A gust of wind shrouded them in snow again, and right at that moment—Now!—Glenda hit the gas pedal and honked the horn once more.

The tires spun a few seconds. The bus crawled ahead slowly and gained speed. Suddenly one tire screeched on a dry pavement patch, and the bus lurched forward too fast.

The deer didn't move. Glenda had hoped they would. All she'd wanted to do was scare them so they'd jump out of the way.

She could drive a bus forever, doomed like a phantom. Though she could play cards with Marlene all the time and never cross the yard and go back home, she'd still feel Frank's eyes gazing into her through the walls between them while he stood by their kitchen sink and looked out the window toward Marlene's house. She pictured him there in his tattered bathrobe with his oxygen tank on a little dolly and the tube wrapped around his leg as it traveled up his body to his nose.

In the few months after the funeral, she'd gotten to know Marlene better than she'd known her in thirty years. Thirty years she knew nobody but Frank and their daughter, which was the way Frank liked it.

The bus knocked the deer down before they had a chance to react. They went under the front bumper with a smack, and they bumped and knocked all along the underside of the bus as Glenda drove over them.

Frank told her to keep driving forward across the bridge. Frank told her to drive slow, careful.

She was still afraid she'd lose control and go over the railing.

She came to the end of the bridge and inched down the icy exit ramp there. She was thankful there were no more entire universes between snowflakes.

She disembarked for the restroom. She didn't dare look underneath the bus.

She stamped snow from the parking lot off her wet shoes, got back in the bus, and continued down the snowy highway.

While she drove, she dreamed of chips and salsa and guacamole, quarters in a little pile on the table next to her cards, Marlene's laugh, and opera soft in the background.

She wished again that the deer had moved out of the way.

Why didn't they? They should have. They would have in another universe. Wouldn't they?

Her hands were clenched tightly on the wheel. The barking CB radio voices were still unintelligible to her. She listened to them regardless.

All of this was so strange to Glenda. Like déjà vu.

She did not believe in déjà vu. She thought déjà vu was simply forgotten micro memories of previous events reminding you they were buried in your brain like the way tiny insects spin tops on a dead pond. Or the way fish noses break ripple circles across the surface and rearrange pollen whorls into new fingerprints.

Glenda took a deep breath of winter air. Suddenly Glenda's body was too warm for her to be in it. Her

regenerating skin cells ignited a surge of heat—like a fuse—
up and down her nerves, a surge that combusted a backdraft
toward Frank, who was standing there in an opened
doorway, his hand on the doorknob.

The ferocious fire incinerated him in a demon-melting
roar until he was just an ashy cloud scattering in the snow
and Glenda was left alone somewhere in the middle of all
those overlapping universes between snowflakes.

"They don't know where to go," she said.

The man in the car mumbled something Glenda could
hear but couldn't understand. A line of cars behind the bus
honked and honked. Glenda would have asked the man to
say it again, but she was too busy being held up by the deer,
too busy figuring this all out, and she didn't care what any
man staying put in a car had to say.

Marlene had a habit of saying, "Do you want to talk to the
man in charge or to the woman who knows what's going
on?" Marlene'd put up a sign on her kitchen wall for that.
The sign was a varnished oak slab, letters carved out and
painted yellow. Marlene hung it above the knife block where
she leaned her cutting boards next to the sink. She'd found
the sign in a pub in Ireland, she told Glenda once, where
townspeople brought their instruments on Wednesday
nights, and fiddles and accordions and penny whistles
whirled and wheeled all evening on the west coast a mile or
so from the ocean, and she'd asked the pubkeeper if she
could have the sign as a souvenir, so the pubkeeper gave it
to her with a free pint of Guinness. Marlene brought the glass
home too, and it still shimmered with faint music far away
down deep inside.

Glenda looked forward to going to Ireland someday, to the very pub where Marlene discovered the sign and received the glass. But she wasn't going anywhere until she got those deer out of the way.

At other times, the snow in her shoes would have been cuffs around her ankles that chained her indecision in place. Tonight was not one of those times. She pulled her feet free from the snow and forced her way toward the center of the bridge.

The two deer perked their ears.

Glenda pulled her zipped coat tighter around her, leaned her head into the wind with her face turned slightly away to keep the snow out of her eyes. She crossed universes and universes in these few seconds it took to make her way those few feet to the center of the bridge where the deer were. She was a shooting star leaving a trail across countless skies in those universes, skies too small for her to see.

The deer's eyes followed her coming. The deer didn't move. It was like the deer were lawn ornaments absurdly positioned out of place. Where they didn't belong.

She didn't belong there either. And maybe that's why the three of them almost connected. Glenda extended her hand. Snowflakes melted immediately after contact on the two deer's brown and pink noses. The two deer inched their noses nearer to her.

Glenda's fingers were just about close enough to touch the first when both animals twanged their legs at the same time. They snapped around, leaped once, twice, three times.

On the opposite edge of the bridge, they stopped and looked back.

Glenda followed as quickly as she could, but by the time she arrived at the opposite end of the bridge they were gone.

Tracks were the only signs they'd been there. Already the wind was covering them.

This hastened Glenda along to the shoulder, down the ditch, and to the edge of the field where the tracks led in parallel lines that disappeared in the dark and snow. Here the snowdrifts were as high as her thighs. Glenda plowed through the first drift and then another, where she lost her footing for a moment. She regained it and surged into the third.

Strange. No longer was she tired.

Wouldn't now be a good time to have the phone, she thought, with a full charged battery.

Look at me, she imagined writing under a selfie she would post.

She didn't know much how to use the phone, but she knew people liked taking pictures of themselves. Her daughter in Tucson sent them all the time. One from the Grand Canyon gave the impression her daughter would fall off the rim with one wrong step.

Glenda didn't tell her daughter this, but she thought the way her daughter's head was tilted back in all her selfies made her look ridiculous. They emphasized her nostrils and the bottom of her front teeth.

Look how all my cells have fully regenerated, Glenda imagined she might write under her own selfie of her running through the snow to drive the deer far away from the bridge, far enough so they'd never go back there.

Look at me saving two deer. Run, little deer, run! Don't

come back to the bridge, little deer. Run far away!

Another hour or two on the road didn't seem quite so discouraging, and going home regenerated to an empty house wasn't quite so lonely.

Not with Marlene for a next-door neighbor.

LONG CHAIN OF REFUSALS

BUT SOMETHING IN THE HORSE was still alive. The moment Grace's rhinestone rainbow bracelet hit the pavement, numerous maculae quickly spread all over the horse from nose to hooves to tail. They were perfectly round spots at first of various colors, but they rose into lumps like candy buttons. Rock salt. Rhinestones.

They were translucent, faceted rhinestones.

They sprouted legs, necks, tails, ears, each rhinestone sprouting just one leg, one neck, one tail, or one ear.

They drew together as if suddenly magnetized and assembled into colorful little horses rearing on hind legs.

Hundreds of little colorful horses — no bigger than crickets — were rearing and neighing. The dead horse — every inch of its honey-brown coat — was bursting and vibrating and quivering with these little colorful horses that had risen from something still alive deep inside. They flashed and sparkled, gathered more rhinestones into themselves, and flourished to the size of the intricately wired rhinestone horses Grace's mother had salvaged from the neighbors' rummage sale.

All at the same time, the horses leapt off. They alighted on the highway, heads high, manes glistening.

The highway was carpeted with the glittering rhinestones wired into the shapes of these horses.

Each horse shifted its weight from one hoof to another. Ears were alert. Several little horses snorted at once, and before Grace could call to them by name—

she knew the name of each horse. how? she had no idea

—they bolted, galloped in all directions away down the ditches, across the fields, over the horizon.

All this happened in less time than it took Grace to let out her breath, less time than it took for a rope of her usual contempt for George to knot her head to her toes.

George and the deputy were engaged in energetic conversation that was silent to Grace—to her, their mouths were moving with no sound. The deputy was hooking his thumbs in his belt. George was gesturing.

Dislodged from their horses like sequins fallen from a gown, only three lone rhinestones remained on the center line painted down the highway. Each shimmered as if absorbing the will to jump, and then they rolled several inches and bounced five or six times, each skip higher than the previous. The last skip was the longest, a take-off. One rhinestone launched toward the deputy, one toward George, and one toward Grace.

George and the deputy apparently never saw the two rhinestones flying toward them. They flinched at the same time and flashed their palms to their faces.

In the half second before George's hand met his eye to

start rubbing it vigorously, Grace's focus sharpened, and his green eye was as large as a moon in hers. A cobalt gelding reared inside the bubble of his vitreous humor. It flared its nostrils. It was looking at her. The look communicated to Grace that George would forever be rubbing his horse-studded eye.

Grace was satisfied for the first time since she didn't know when.

She asked herself what color the deputy's new eye horse might be. Gold?

Gold in black would look nice, she thought.

It was her turn to instinctively reach up to swat away the last rhinestone still curving toward her face. She didn't want to — how nice it would be to have a horse of her own in her eye — but the reflex was too strong to arrest.

Fortunately, she missed. But her right eye stung. That surprised her.

She had no time to be disappointed because the sting was pushed away by a massive bloom of rosy light that for the rest of her life, whenever her view shifted to that eye, colored her world with a soothing, blushing warmth.

**SPEED
LIMIT
55**

BAD MANNERS ARE BETTER THAN NO MANNERS AT ALL

"Life, friends, is boring. We must not say so."

— John Berryman

MAYFIELD BROWN WAS TOO OLD and too far from love for those lips to be following him around.

Nothing like this had ever happened to him. The lips puckered up as if they were moving in to kiss him and opened and closed like little red butterflies. A hundred of them, he estimated. Disembodied. They bounced in the air, flew and looped everywhere, and left red trails glowing behind that lingered a few seconds before they disappeared.

They made the already stuffy and dark room feel hotter. This discomfort along with the lip light kept Mayfield from falling asleep, which irked him because he was leaving on his trip with Yokley tomorrow and wanted to catch up on the rest he'd lost tossing and turning these past few nights.

He couldn't catch the lips. They'd been following him for three days. Tonight they darted above the bed. The glow from the red trails was brighter than the face of the alarm clock on the nightstand. He reached out and grabbed for a pair of lips that looked fuller and more luscious than the rest, but it slipped through his fingers. It stopped just beyond his reach, puckered and smacked at him, and flittered on with the others.

A pair of lips swooped down toward his foot. It puckered up against his sole and kissed it. In a few seconds, the bottom of his foot started to itch. He tried to scratch it with the big toe of his other foot, but he only succeeded in tickling himself.

So he stopped.

Soon the bottom of his other foot started to itch. He threw aside the sweat-soaked sheets, sat up, put his feet off the bed, and rubbed them back and forth on the carpet until they were hot and stinging.

It wasn't yet light out, but he showered.

The lips showered in the cold water with him, somersaulting like happy kids in a sprinkler.

Soon after toweling dry, Mayfield was sweating again, but he dressed in his usual button-down shirt and tie. He tightened the knot and adjusted it, and his wife's voice played in his head what she'd told him every morning, that he dressed like an Ivy League kid.

She told him every morning that he looked as if he'd just gotten off his bicycle.

Mayfield had made the choice every morning to remain oblivious to that.

He checked his hair one more time in the living room's gilded mirror, where the huge cranberry chandelier hung.

The new windows were open. The chandelier crystals tinkled in the summer dawn and dashed little rainbows around the walls.

It hung all the way down to the living room floor and took up just about all the central space in the room. It had been a product of his wife's obsession with cranberry-colored glass. Every time she saw a cranberry piece — a saucer in an antique shop, a cup in a café, a carafe at a flea market — she either bought it after dickering for it or quickly slipped it into the oversize black knock-off purse she always carried.

A harmless enough hobby, not too expensive, but sometimes Mayfield wished she'd dicker just a little longer on the pricier pieces she couldn't sneak into her purse.

Mayfield's back ached on account of not sleeping well. One of his teeth throbbed. He was tired and not sure he wanted to leave today.

A worn olive couch was settling against one wall, and a vintage television on a wobbly cart leaned against the opposite. The chandelier was between them.

Mayfield sagged in the couch for a while and watched the rainbows and the lips whirling around the room. The sun climbed high enough so it didn't shine in the new windows anymore or cast fleeting rainbows through the crystals. Mayfield tried to understand a game show while he watched it through the chandelier.

one day she smashed a cup in the kitchen sink, laughed in glee —
this was the only time mayfield remembered ever seeing her

laugh — and proceeded to smash everything else she'd collected until the sink, counter, and floor looked like a cranberry ice storm had raged through the kitchen

SPEED
LIMIT
55

A WEATHER BULLETIN sandwiched between two pharmaceutical commercials ("...side effects may include...") announced that livestock was succumbing all across the Midwest and the South to the punishing drought. According to the grim-faced weatherman, no end was in sight.

One pair of lips hovered an inch from the screen in front of the weatherman's red bow tie while the weatherman was talking.

The remaining lips fluttered between all the strands of the chandelier's diamond-shaped crystals. When the weather alert ended and a soothing-voice pharmaceutical commercial started, the pair of lips that was distracted by the red bow tie rejoined the others.

A court show's credits were rolling by the time Mayfield's neighbor Yokley Tribble peered in from the porch through the narrow window next to the door. He rang the bell.

Mayfield let him in.

Yokley was thin, just a little over five feet tall, and unmarried, which he blamed on his height. His clothes — fern-green jogging pants and a blue T-shirt with an erupting volcano on the chest — were a size too small for him.

But Mayfield wasn't sure if Yokley's sweatshirt had a volcano on it or a tornado. The ash cloud looked like a funnel cloud. The mountain looked like dirt flying. Volcano or tornado? Mayfield didn't know. A tornado would be an odd choice—some folks in the neighborhood were still fixing damage from the last one.

Then again, Yokley *was* odd.

Mayfield took Yokley's stained and tattered topcoat, which was a little wet as if caught outside at the start of a storm. Its belt dragged from one loop. He put it in the closet and poured Yokley a cup of Bengal Spice iced tea.

Yokley sat on the olive couch. Puddles collected on and soaked into the threadbare auburn carpet under his shoes.

Mayfield sat next to him. "Is it raining finally?" Mayfield said.

Yokley looked in his glass after a sip. "It's like drinking refrigerated gingerbread," he said.

Mayfield waited a minute in silence for an answer he didn't receive to his question about rain. He wanted to know because he couldn't remember the last time it had rained. It had been a long, dry, hot, and dusty summer. Mayfield's house was old, without air conditioning because the unit in the kitchen window was broken, and Mayfield didn't want to bounce a check buying a new one. He didn't recall the forecast calling for a break in the drought today—

"...no end in sight..."

wasn't that what the weatherman said?

—but Mayfield was more disturbed and worried by Yokley's apparent obliviousness to the flying lips everywhere.

He thought Yokley's blue eyes looked sad and distant through his thick glasses. White hair curled down over his forehead. His rare smile this morning that had gone yellow like old paper over the years suggested genuine interest, however, in anything Mayfield might have to say.

This told Mayfield that Yokley hadn't heard the rain question. He let it go.

But Mayfield decided to hold off on asking him if he could see the lips. He didn't want his friend thinking the heat had made him crazy.

Then again, wearing a tie in heat like this *was* crazy.

Perhaps he only needed to phrase the question correctly.

Mayfield cleared his throat and took a deep breath. "Do you see anything unusual?"

The TV was now whispering a soap opera through the chandelier. A woman with big blond hair threw her arms around a pompadour gentleman in a suit and kissed him hard.

Yokley finished his tea in one last gulp and handed the glass back to Mayfield. "Your chandelier is still too big for this room."

Mayfield balanced the glass on his armrest.

Yokley leaned forward and reached for a string of crystals. He tugged it. The chandelier swayed a little.

The lips changed direction in big arcs around it and gave it room to swing.

"The mail usually comes around noon," Yokley said. "Soon as it's here we can leave."

"What did you buy now?"

"Remember the episode where they found crates of costumes and movie cameras on the bottom of the lagoon?"

Mayfield had to admit that he didn't.

The lips stopped suddenly, suspended in the air, and

puckered up as if eavesdropping on something they weren't supposed to hear.

"It's a gown she wore on that episode, complete with matching shoes and earrings. Seller says those shoes are pristine, not a scuff on them. He says when he first got them there was a little sand from the soundstage still in them. He saved it in a baggie for me."

Mayfield suddenly was irritated that Yokley hadn't said anything about the lips, which by now had recommenced their Peter Pan zooming. Another warm draft came through the open windows, and the cranberry chandelier made a rustling, clinkering noise. A lip pair fell onto the armrest by the glass, opening and closing as if gasping for air. It faded slowly and disappeared.

This didn't really surprise Mayfield. He was starting not even to notice the lips in the daytime. It was the nights that were the worst.

Rather than snap in irritation at Yokley, Mayfield took the glass to the kitchen. He refrained from expressing annoyance about the moisture ring it had left on the armrest.

The kitchen seemed smaller now that Meredith was no longer in it. The glass-fronted cabinets where she'd stored her cranberry dishes were empty. Pots and pans of all sizes and shapes hung from the ceiling. The dirty yellow linoleum was cracked. The kitchen smelled of long-damp towels and lemon dishwashing soap.

SPEED
LIMIT
55

THE LIPS FOLLOWED Mayfield and Yokley to the mall,

where Yokley said he had to stop before they gathered his mail and hit the road. Yokley parked his pickup truck in a handicapped spot. He tracked wet footprints across the parking lot.

Mayfield welcomed the frigid blast that blew through the parting automatic doors when they entered, though the lips appeared to shiver and purse together. He was worried people would think he looked like he was wearing a system of miniature neon freeways, red cars buzzing up and down, round and round him.

But the few shoppers didn't seem to pay him any mind. He wanted to know why. He asked himself over and over how they could possibly not see the lips.

While Yokley was off shopping, Mayfield browsed a display of gold bracelets marked 75% off in the window of a jewelry store. Meredith had never asked for anything like that. Maybe she really had wanted jewelry but just never said so. Mayfield understood just then how one could miss even the detestable things about someone.

Mayfield kept Meredith's picture on the wall above the vintage TV back home. Most of the time, he was able to ignore it because she glared from the picture, her face blank and pinched, her lips squeezed together in a long frown that looked as if someone had drawn a curved line on the picture from one end of her face to the other. Her hair was up in a tight little bun.

Meredith's mountainous cranberry chandelier was a three-dimensional bead curtain between her picture and Mayfield. Every night, Mayfield's boredom blurred the room, and the cranberry diamond crystals melted into the same plane as the picture. Two diamond crystals stood out in particular—right where Meredith's eyes should have been, she now had two cranberry-colored diamonds glittering at him. With that image of his wife's eyes—what color had they really been before, he wondered—he nodded off with the TV on and, these past few nights, his wife's picture framed in looping lips.

The last few years of marriage had been ones of more arguments than usual, the most common being her desire to be cremated versus Mayfield's desire to be buried.

"You will cremate me," Meredith said.

"I would rather bury you," Mayfield said.

"You will not."

"Why are you going to care?" Mayfield said.

"If you go against my wishes—"

"You'll be dead," Mayfield said.

"I do not want to be buried."

"Why?"

"Mark my words, my ghost will come back and haunt you forever."

"You're an atheist," Mayfield said.

"I believe in my ghost!" Meredith shouted.

Most people who ended up witnessing this argument, which always played out exactly the same way, assumed it was a comical dynamic between them, but it was dead serious, so serious that Mayfield, to whoever was caught as a witness, whether in the grocery store or the doctor's waiting room or in the art museum, said, "She's going to—I just know it—she's going to cremate me."

while she smashed smashed smashed, he added up the cost in his head, stood there a little concerned but more dumbfounded and watched her raise her arms high over her, hands clutching a saucer or a cup or a carafe, and hurl it explosively down, one after another, so loud that the clashing and tinkling sounds of both the glass and his mental cash register rang in his ears long into the night after she'd smashed everything and she lay in bed by his side, breathing softly

SPEED LIMIT 55

YOKLEY'S STRANGE-FAMILIAR voice eventually called Mayfield's name. Mayfield skimmed his eyes over the small crowd of sullen shoppers hauling bulging paper bags crinkling from stretched handles.

Yokley emerged toward him. New sneakers gleamed white and drew attention to his feet under his jogging pants. He carried a naked mannequin horizontally, his arms around its waist. A stainless-steel support rod and stand were tied to the mannequin's back. The mannequin's legs were still posed parallel, but its arms were cocked apart in a power walker's swing, and its head was turned downward, its long red hair dangling and dragging on the floor.

His topcoat belt trailing behind him and the mannequin carried as if it were a pole, Yokley looked like a bizarre tightrope walker.

Shoppers gawked and pointed.

What was most odd, Mayfield thought, was the coat was

still streaked with raindrops, and it hadn't rained at all.

"Let's load up this doll and get some lunch" Yokley said.

Mayfield took the mannequin by the ankles—"Careful now," Yokley said, "so you don't pull it all to pieces"—and helped Yokley carry it through the mall and out to the pickup. He ignored the people staring at them.

The lips all descended and settled on the mannequin's legs to ride like nesting swallows.

Out in the parking lot, Yokley dropped the tailgate, sat on it, and hefted himself up backwards. He steadied himself, unfolded a blanket, and spread it on the rusty truck bed.

Mayfield stood and watched him, thinking again that maybe he didn't want to spend the next few weeks riding around in the truck with Yokley. Mayfield had one hand on the mannequin's back to keep it from falling down. Its hair blew in his eyes, and his other hand brushed it away.

Yokley hooked his arms through the mannequin's and pulled. Mayfield helped him lift it up, and Yokley was careful to not let it drop. He arranged it, head near the cab, feet near the tailgate, until he was satisfied and wrapped the blanket around it. He tucked it under the mannequin, hopped down, and swung the tailgate up.

Mayfield's reluctance to embark on a cross-country road trip with Yokley mounted when Yokley turned into traffic directly in front of a speeding car that shortly blared its horn. Yokley appeared oblivious, and Mayfield argued with himself the next mile or so about whether or not he should have said something. Mayfield lately, though, had been so bored with the tedium of never-ending days and longer nights that he wished some catastrophe would happen, maybe one featuring fire engines, police cars, and guns.

We're glad Georgia's boring you out of your mind, Mayfield was not long ago saying to empty rooms.

The lips were such an unforeseen answer.

The bakery truck alongside Yokley's pickup soon pulled forward and merged ahead of them, and the car Yokley had cut off zoomed around.

The lips were up ahead, flying along the road as if guiding the way. Cars and trucks passed through them. Mayfield and Yokley rode in quiet until they got off the freeway. Movie complexes went by, and some oil change places all on the same block. A custard stand and a revolving sign flashing. The drug store where Mayfield got his prescriptions filled. The funeral home where Meredith had been embalmed and displayed and taken away four months ago, now closed down and shut up, a For Sale sign in front.

Mayfield wouldn't have given her funeral another thought — passing by the funeral home would have been as ordinary as the car wash — if not for the fact that the check he wrote and handed across the glossy black desk to the undertaker still hadn't cleared the bank.

Mayfield had regarded his reflection in the undertaker's desk and felt as if he were looking at himself shining on the surface of an underground lake at the end of a cavern, lit up from behind by a flashlight, and that was the only moment of grief he felt during that week of phone calls, visitors from out of town, handshaking, platitudes, hash brown casseroles and Jell-O salads from the neighbors taking over his kitchen.

Yokley called the hash brown casseroles bosom casseroles.

SPEED
LIMIT
55

water so calm and smooth and clear while he pulled her body in over slippery rocks that a million moon faces and fish faces and meredith faces grinned howled snickered frowned jeered at him, faces that were just under the surface yet a thousand miles under

SPEED
LIMIT
55

THE UNDERTAKER'S DESK was the same color as the rotary-dial phone at home that he called the bank with every morning inquiring about the check after he learned the funeral home went out of business, which he also found odd because he'd never heard of a funeral home going out of business. Didn't they change hands? Get passed down from father to son?

The need to bury never went away, did it?

The phone in the corner of his cluttered desk in the back room of his house was so black and shone so brightly even the smudged fingerprints on the handset gleamed. Every morning, Mayfield brushed aside some papers next to the phone, picked up a pen and the handset. He dialed the number for the bank, listened to all the options he could select if he had a push-tone phone, and waited for an operator.

He tapped the pen on the desk and brushed some papers around some more.

When a familiar-sounding operator came on, he asked the same question he'd asked every morning the past few months.

Had the check cleared yet?

Mayfield heard keyboard keys clicking on the other end. When the woman told him no in a voice he thought sounded terse and irritated, Mayfield sighed, thanked her, and hung up. She hadn't asked today if he wanted to order a stop payment on it.

Every morning after this conversation, Mayfield stood, stretched his back, drifted to the living room, and sagged into the olive couch.

At the moment, riding past the building in Yokley's pickup, Mayfield was grabbed by a desire to obtain the desk. He couldn't explain these odd impulses to own something that didn't belong to him, but they started the day after Meredith's burial when he was studying two paintings in his doctor's waiting room. He was surrounded by a coughing mob, and, in a spate of dizziness, he stood up without thinking and stole one off the wall.

The one that Mayfield did not steal was an impressionist style of a bull and an old woman gathering hay. He wanted to ask someone in the waiting room if bulls ate hay. He fixed his eye on the red handkerchief tied around the woman's head in the painting.

The painting was an original, not a print. The handkerchief was the only red splash in green, yellow, and brown oils. Even the sky in the painting was the same green and brown as the ground.

Mayfield found it only moderately beautiful, except for the red handkerchief, which stoked a flare of danger in his heart and a pump of energy in his legs. He imagined the moment after the one captured in the painting. He pictured the bull snorting and stamping and the woman wheeling just in time out of the way of its horns, her long green and brown skirts swishing like a cape.

The second painting, the one Mayfield did steal, was downright ugly. Mayfield found it distasteful, especially for a doctor's office. A red blob and purple tendrils. The tendrils stretched across the canvas in all directions. Mayfield thought it looked like a placenta dropped on a white floor.

But he had to take that one.

No one paid any attention to him lift the painting off the nail it hung from, and no one stopped him going out the door with it. He pumped his legs to his car and played in his mind a productive and fulfilling future career as an art thief.

That morning had been the first time in his life that Mayfield was scared of his own death and of no one coming to his memorial service. Maybe that explained the thrill he felt stealing something for the first time after years enabling his wife stealing her cranberry pieces.

It was just as well that Mayfield didn't have many friends nearby. When one has no friends, one has no need to entertain them, and when one has no need to entertain, stolen art can garnish walls undetected, and cranberry chandeliers can hang without criticism because no one comes over for cocktails, cheese plates, and teriyaki-marinated chicken strips on sticks.

Mayfield's future stolen art would certainly never consist of any masterpieces, however. The connecting rooms in his old bungalow on the edge of town by the lake that was drying up more every day would be cluttered with nondescript watercolors and abstract oils from waiting rooms, thrift stores, and hotel lobbies.

But because the painting he took from his doctor's waiting room wasn't one he'd ever display in his house, he broke the wooden frame the canvas was stapled to, folded the disgusting artwork in half, and stuffed it later in the trash can at the front door of the diner he went to for lunch.

The same diner, beckoning a cozy green and yellow, that Yokley was now turning toward.

Somewhere along the way, the blanket Yokley had wrapped around the mannequin had flown out the back of the pickup. The mannequin's hair was windblown over its face. The mannequin had shifted so that the tailgate pushed its bare feet and painted toenails up.

Mayfield wondered if the blanket flying out had caused any swerves or accidents. If he was driving and a blanket billowed and rolled his way, he might have driven right into it, taken a chance on the fate of not seeing where he was going.

Because that's what his life wanted him to do now.

They left the mannequin and went inside. They sat there about a half hour, sipping their coffee and waiting for the waiter to come back and take their food order. Yokley sucked on a drinking straw and shakily held it as if it were a cigarette.

The lips hovered around Mayfield's head as if resting or waiting for a command. Mayfield felt like a beekeeper wearing a netted hat. He ignored the lips as best as he could.

The conversation trailed off, and, fighting the urge to swat the lips away, Mayfield said, "Why not collect Marilyn Monroe's dresses? Why this old sitcom star's dresses?" What he'd really wanted to say, however, was *Did you ever buy jewelry for your wife,* but it came out *Why not collect Marilyn Monroe's dresses.*

He remembered Yokley had never married. Yokley blamed that on his height.

Yokley raised his eyebrows, stirred his coffee, and brought his mug to his mouth. He took a long drink, set his mug down, said "Marilyn's are too expensive," and took a wet, empty drag from the straw. He drummed his fingers on the table, turned around, and looked long and sad out the window at traffic. His shoulders under his rain-streaked topcoat deflated, and he sighed. His face looked like the back of an elephant. Droopy nose. Sagging cheeks.

Mayfield had come to know two frequent expressions that were typical of Yokley. The first was of someone noticing and looking at—really looking at—a tree for the first time, mouth open, eyebrows furrowed, crooked jam-jar glasses about to fall off the nose, eyes following the trunk and the branches up and up and then studying each leaf.

The second was a look of disgust and annoyance, one of finding a dead cockroach in the flour, and this was the look Yokley practiced most often because he was judgmental of everybody and everything.

Mayfield almost vocalized a request to backtrack to the funeral home and rattle the doors to check if one was unlocked. Or perhaps pry up a window.

The pickup bed was large enough for the desk and the mannequin. How funny it would be if they could swipe a chair and seat the mannequin in it. Mayfield pictured the naked mannequin's hair flying in the wind and laughed.

"You aren't the first who has thought my hobby is strange," Yokley said.

"That's not what I was laughing at," Mayfield said.

Yokley didn't ask for elaboration so Mayfield let it go. He wasn't sure now that hauling the desk home was a good idea — lifting, carrying, porch stairs, tight corners — but, for the first time, he was somewhat excited about hitting the road and stealing stuff with Yokley, who had confessed he'd started the habit too shortly before Meredith died.

The waiter never came to take their food order. He was nowhere in the diner, far as Mayfield could see.

Mayfield unscrewed the salt and pepper shakers and poured their contents into his coffee cup, where an inch of coffee remained. He stirred it up, screwed the tops back on, and stuffed the shakers in a pocket. He swept the silverware off the table and collected it all in a bundle, which went in another pocket. He found a place under his shirt for the ketchup bottle.

He and Yokley left without paying for the coffee. They escaped unnoticed in a cloud of lips.

Out on the highway, a line of lips settled on Mayfield's navy tie. Mayfield brushed them off, and they hurtled out with the airflow through the pickup's open window like bugs. Maybe if Yokley drove fast enough, Mayfield thought, the rest of the lips wouldn't be able to keep up.

But keep up they did in a swarm puckering alongside next to the truck. Mayfield threw the ketchup bottle at them. The swarm formed a ring the bottle flew through. Mayfield tossed out the salt and pepper shakers and the silverware piece by piece for a mile or so, but, each time, the swarm formed a ring that the salt and pepper shakers and silverware pieces flew through, and Mayfield felt like he was winning a bizarre carnival game.

If he was puzzled by Mayfield tossing everything he'd taken out the window, Yokley didn't say anything about it.

SPEED
LIMIT
55

YOKLEY'S PORCH LOOKED as if it would fall down any second. It had the shape of an asthmatic's mouth mid wheeze. A flat box, corner crushed in, sat near the front door like a crashed balsa glider.

Yokley hopped down from the cab and ran up his weedy walk to fetch it. His foot went through the middle step, but he didn't slow down — he had the box under his arm and was back at the cab in no time.

"Can you help me with the mannequin?" he said to Mayfield. He coughed.

He coughed again.

Again.

Mayfield hauled in the mannequin while Yokley coughed a few more times, pounded his chest, caught his breath. The lips followed of course and, once inside Yokley's kitchen, collected on the mannequin's hair like a teased wig.

His eyes still watery from his coughing fit, Yokley carefully sliced through the tape, opened the box, and lifted out a folded dress wrapped in tissue paper and tied with string. Yokley peeled the paper off and held the dress up so it fell open.

Silver and gold lamé.

Mayfield supported the mannequin with his arms around its waist and watched Yokley step around the spartan kitchen, the sparkly dress against his body as if modeling it.

The kitchen was spotless. Not a crumb or sticky spot anywhere. The contrast with the overgrown and neglected yard amused Mayfield. So did Yokley pirouetting around the austere kitchen with the tinsel-twinkle dress.

Yokley gathered the dress and buried his face in it. He took a deep, rattling breath, held it, let it out. He looked at Mayfield and smiled old paper at him as if regarding a lover.

"Perfume," Yokley said. "My God, Mayfield, you can still smell her perfume."

And he thrust the dress at Mayfield.

Mayfield let go the mannequin to take it. This disturbed the lips and launched them around the room like a glitter bomb. Several bounced off his face and Yokley's. Mayfield brushed at them, but Yokley only reacted to the falling mannequin. He grabbed it before it fell and propped it with a clatter against the counter.

Mayfield sniffed the dress. He detected no perfume, just a faint basement musty scent. For Mayfield this scent conjured a sense of the past, of a long time ago, of darkness, of packed away and forgotten, of no desire to be unearthed. All perfumes metamorphose to mildew like they are supposed to, so where was Yokley's mind? How far back was it probing to pull the past into the present, to report perfume from mildew? It was Mr. Hyde transforming back to Dr. Jekyll. Lou Ferrigno back to Bill Bixby. Monstrous vermin back to Gregor Samsa.

Not long ago, when Meredith was alive, Mayfield

dismissed any kind of philosophy as ridiculous. But lately he'd been philosophizing in a way that made him, for the first time in his life, feel important. He didn't delude himself into believing he was the first to ever think these thoughts, and he didn't know who Mr. Hyde, Dr. Jekyll, and Gregor Samsa were — he'd only heard Yokley talking about them as if they were somehow paramount to his living and breathing. Nevertheless, thinking this way was a welcome boost to an intellect Mayfield never felt he had before.

And he'd developed a new habit of stealing cheap art and trinkets, just like his wife had, and it was a kind of fun he'd never had before either.

He had Yokley to thank for that because Yokley started it first.

Mayfield thought all this while his neighbor set up the mannequin on the stand, wiped it down with a damp towel, and pulled the dress past its waist and down its legs.

Mayfield agreed silently that it was a beautiful dress. Two silver sequined strips marked an X across the bust.

The dress seemed to him to hang a little loosely on the mannequin, however, but he hesitated to point that out to Yokley.

Yokley stroked the mannequin's hair smooth and adjusted its arms so that one dropped a hand to the mannequin's thigh and the other hung behind. This, coupled with one foot in front of the other, gave the mannequin the air of stopping at the end of a runway and posing, gaze off somewhere far away.

When Yokley stepped back, his head high, his hands on his hips to study it, the lips all did the same. Somehow they puckered and pursed so as to look like they were also studying, like their hands were also on their hips.

"It fits perfect," Yokley said. "Perfect! What are the odds it would fit so perfect?"

"Where are the shoes?" Mayfield said.

The lips turned to face him.

Yokley's eyes froze wide. "The shoes!"

The lips turned to regard Yokley once more as Yokley seized the box and shook it upside down.

But it was empty. A few silent seconds passed. Yokley stood there staring into the box.

The lips all frowned.

"The earrings!" Yokley said. He frisked through the tissue paper and tossed each sheet aloft as if the earrings might be under one.

The lips dodged the sinking sheets, but one sheet wafted down on a pair of lips that wasn't quick enough, and that pair jerked around like a flailing ghost trying to shake it off.

The lips all laughed.

"The shoes!" Yokley's eyes remained wide. "The earrings!" His jaw hung.

Mayfield didn't know what to suggest.

After a few more seconds standing that way staring at Mayfield, Yokley ripped the return address label from the box flap. He held it toward Mayfield.

Valentine, Nebraska.

"We'll stop by and pick them up ourselves," Yokley said.

Mayfield offered that maybe the shoes and earrings were coming in another box and would arrive tomorrow.

"Always a day away," Yokley said.

The lips all sighed.

"Tomorrow, and tomorrow, and tomorrow," Yokley said.

SPEED
LIMIT
55

THEY DROVE WITH no itinerary, no reservations, no confirmation numbers. Just headed north on the backroads out of town after Yokley faced the mannequin toward the side door in the kitchen and explained that the fake face would scare anyone peeping in. He would put it in the granny flat out back with the others when he returned, he said. He packed a duffle bag full of clothes and another duffle bag full of worn paperbacks, and Mayfield popped back home next door to take his tie off —

too hot

— and collect his bag too.

Mayfield withdrew a thousand dollars from his bank, rolled the bills, and stuffed his front pocket. The funeral home check, wherever it was — out there somewhere, in a drawer, or under a desk, dropped and forgotten wherever checks written to pay for funerals go when funeral homes suddenly shut down — was in danger of bouncing now, but Mayfield wasn't going to worry about that until the trip was over.

Nothing much to do the first hour or two on the road. The radio was tuned to a jazz station. The windows were up. Yokley had the air conditioner running full blast. Maybe it would help his coughing, he'd said.

The scenery was too familiar to enjoy, so Mayfield nodded off while Yokley drove, and a pebble kicked up by the car ahead cracked the windshield.

SPEED
LIMIT
55

the smashing again, and again, then the broken glass left blanketing everything in the kitchen, and she went right to bed without sweeping it up, the chandelier in the living room the only thing not smashed

SPEED
LIMIT
55

THE SCENERY WAS strange and new by the time Mayfield felt alert enough to keep his eyes open. He asked Yokley if they'd be going through Toomsboro.

"Maybe after Andalusia," Yokley said. A cough stopped his sentence like a period.

They arrived in downtown Milledgeville, where Yokley parked the truck crooked. They ordered a pepperoni pizza and two bottles of root beer at a pizzeria by the college. Mayfield brushed a few pairs of lips off his food because they settled on the pizza like pepperoni.

Mayfield paid the bill with a crisp fifty, and they set off north past the shopping mall, a couple motels, a furniture store, and the splattered, fly-matted carcass of an animal killed in the middle of the road.

A left turn into an inconspicuous dirt driveway through an open gate. The woods were full with dry pecan and magnolia trees that looked as if they were waiting for fire. The tires crunched on the bone-dry ground up the hill and around a bend. A little ways more, the house and its red metal roof, red brick chimneys and front steps, and long white porch rose before them suddenly like a wreck where a wreck didn't belong.

Yokley drove around to the back and parked next to another white pickup by the water tower.

His abrupt stop caught the lips off guard. They kept going, skidded to a stop, and doubled back to join Mayfield.

Better thieves would have slipped in quiet and fast, Mayfield thought, and disappeared in a moment before anyone had a chance to notice anything out of the ordinary. He was worried Yokley was going to do everything wrong.

They walked the grounds first, Yokley springy and excited in his rain-spattered coat and Mayfield always several steps behind.

Mayfield had already dismissed the rain spots on Yokley's coat as stains that looked wet. The sunlight was hazy and white as it is only in Georgia, so surely any rain spots would have dried off the coat by now.

Mayfield had also come to grips with the fact that only he could see the lips that surrounded him like dragonflies. He no longer worried about attracting attention because they were invisible to everyone else. The other day, Yokley had been talking about animals that could see infrared that humans couldn't, and Mayfield asked himself if maybe he'd developed extra efficiency in his vision that allowed him to detect what had always remained unseen.

That had to be it. One day they weren't there, and one day they were, like the cataract Meredith suddenly complained about at Sunday brunch a few years before she died.

Yokley took a picture of the cow barn and another of

Mayfield posing halfway up its rickety ladder, where a sign clearly commanded him to stay off. Mayfield held on to the ladder with one hand and swung one foot out, and he hoped the wooden rung he was standing on would not give before the shutter clicked.

Mayfield was curious. Would the lips show up on the photos? No way to tell yet because Yokley's camera was an old point-and-shoot loaded with film he'd ordered online.

They wandered some more and remarked on all the red and black DANGER signs posted in front of the crumbling cottages and sheds scattered around the property.

A black snake retreated into tall grass. Mayfield wanted to walk down the mowed path to the pond—they were spending all this time looking around anyway—but Yokley was coughing again. His cheeks were flushed, and his eyes ran. He leaned on a stump by the water pump and fanned his face with his hands. His new sneakers were now red with dirt.

And they'd not left any puddles.

Mayfield suggested they go inside. Something strange and unseen (feathers?) brushed his arm as he went up the red brick steps of the screened porch, and once he was on the porch the feeling of feathers touching his arm disappeared.

He waited for Yokley to pull himself up the white-painted railing past the row of rocking chairs and through the front door, where Mayfield pointed at the Mastercard, Discover, Visa, and American Express stickers and Yokley coughed and wheezed more.

Yokley caught his breath again and said, "We have work to do."

There was no one to welcome them, so they took their time exploring freely. Yokley, his cough now gone, snapped several pictures, a careless thing for a thief to do, but Mayfield felt a calming sense of security too in the old house. He didn't know much about it — Yokley had said it belonged to a famous dead author Mayfield had never heard of — but somehow it communicated to Mayfield everything he needed to know about that writer through its whispered sweet nothings of sequestration, chastity, and disfigurement.

What was suddenly strange, however, after knowing everything he needed to know about the writer from her house, was his inability to picture her alive in her bathrobe with her coffee-spiked Coca-Cola and gassy disappointment, her body drooping and falling apart in rooms that were now photo opportunities presented in a museum-scented, dust-suspended time bubble.

And he was surprised to see Andalusia was a time bubble that time continued to ravage. Deep cracks parted the wall of the staircase. Wallpaper peeled and rolled, and paint flaked in the bedrooms. Curtains hung yellow and tattered upstairs.

In the gift shop, Yokley picked up bumper stickers and books, examined them, and put them back down, leaving everything in disarray on the display tables.

"Fingerprints," Mayfield said quietly, but Yokley went on touching everything.

Mayfield moved toward the front door again. He'd passed the bedroom on the way into the house without looking in, so he stood now in the doorway, which was the first on the left after entering the house from the porch. He stared at the typewriter and crutches. He was especially drawn to the crutches. They leaned against a tall, darkly varnished armoire in the center of the room.

The lips—they'd gone unnoticed by Mayfield too for the short time he was ambling from room to room—now made an arrow above the crutches that pointed down at them.

He moved a little more into the room to get closer, but the yellow rope cordoning it off from the entryway kept him back. A mild jolt sparked from that rope through Mayfield's pants and tightened into a humming thread deep inside his legs.

A cough from Yokley echoed off the hardwood floors.

"Did you see the self-portrait with the pheasant cock anywhere?" Yokley asked.

They'd gone through the house room by room but hadn't located it. Mayfield said he'd be right back and, escorted by the lips, swept through the whole house once more, starting in the back room, through the kitchen and dining room to the gift shop, off to the parlor and up the stairs.

He paused at the window of a bedroom up there that looked out back to the water tower and down to Yokley's truck parked next to the other truck. The raggedy, faded curtains rustled with his breathing. From up in this bedroom, Yokley's truck looked small, too small to believe it carried them the hundred miles from home to this old dairy farm, one micro pinpoint on a massive globe to another. Mayfield stood there thinking of maps when he should have been scouting for Yokley's painting.

Maps and their wide red lines for Interstates.

Thin gray lines for back roads.

If roads were built to scale the way they were drawn on maps, they'd be a mile wide, he thought.

Mayfield hadn't traveled much. He'd wanted to when he was young. He'd imagined a fantastical future for himself, looked forward to his life as a series of globetrotting adventures and a large map of the world taped to his wall with hundreds of colored pushpins in it, the countries with no pushpins entreating him for plane tickets and a backpack.

But he got married. Meredith was a homebody who disintegrated into a nervous wreck any time he brought up the subject of leaving town even for just a weekend. Psychologists had a word for that, but Mayfield couldn't recall it.

This was, Mayfield realized, the farthest he'd been away from home since before their wedding.

Mayfield went back down the stairs to Yokley, who was waiting in the entryway next to the yellow rope restricting access to the bedroom. Mayfield turned his palms up at Yokley and said he couldn't find the self-portrait.

"It has to be here," Yokley said in an unusually quiet, whispery voice.

"The bedroom is the most likely place," Mayfield said. He squatted and wriggled under the yellow rope. He straightened up on the other side and walked over to a barrister bookcase opposite the foot of the bed. A painting of a black woman in overalls, her hands at her sides, rested on top of the bookcase and leaned against the wall.

"What about this one?" Mayfield said.

Yokley didn't answer. His head was cocked in the direction of the gift shop up the hall.

"Is it hers?" Mayfield said.

He shrugged at Mayfield, eyes squinting and showing impatience and panic.

Impatience and panic ignited in Mayfield too—the lips also gasped open—when a man's voice reached his ears from the back of the house. It echoed at first and was followed by what sounded like a screen door slamming.

The lips were scrambling all over the bedroom and bumping into each other like a crowd rushing for a fire exit.

The voice grew louder as it moved into the house, and footsteps now rolled over the hardwood floors.

Mayfield raised his arms for the painting, but he was too short to reach it. The lips started shaking back and forth as if they were heads warning him to stop.

Mayfield searched around for something to stand on, but the corner chair backed with red velvet was too far away and would take precious seconds to drag across the floor.

Rocking the bookcase to topple the painting might damage it if Mayfield couldn't catch it.

Mayfield decided to take the advice from the arrow the lips had made earlier. He left the painting and bolted around the bed toward the crutches instead.

They'd be a more impressive souvenir of their visit, one for him and one for Yokley, though they'd never be able to show them off—

"Why, yes, this is one of her crutches, really!"

—and he gathered them in his arms, leaped for the door, and scooted under the yellow rope right into Yokley's skeletal legs.

Mayfield lost his balance, flailed his arms and the

crutches, and knocked a black-and-white Jesus picture off the wall next to the stairs. Jesus in his white robes, pointing at the heart on the outside of his chest as if it were a medal, fell face down and clattered across the floor.

Yokley folded like an empty cloak on the lower steps of the staircase.

A vase holding several peacock feathers spilled and cracked.

"Let's move," Mayfield said.

Yokley rose up with an urgent ease, light as paper in an updraft.

Through the door and down the steps Mayfield went with the crutches faster than he'd ever gone in his life. Outside on the grassy red dirt, he turned around for Yokley.

Yokley missed the last step and tripped to his knees and palms. His camera went skipping and spinning across the grass.

Whoever the voice belonged to would be coming through the front door any moment and catch them and probably shout at them as the screen slammed, and they'd be in a whole heap of trouble. Mayfield sprinted to Yokley's pickup, which was now covered lightly in red dirt, and threw the crutches in the back with the duffel bags.

When he got in the driver's seat, a hot flash of worry stormed through his mind. Where were—

pray to God not in Yokley's pocket

—the keys?

In the ignition.

Mayfield started the truck and raced it around the water pump, past the house, and toward Yokley, who was in the same spot in front of the porch, staring at another man leaping from the steps toward him.

Mayfield floored it while reaching across the cab to open the passenger door. In a perfect sequence of synchronized motions, the truck began speeding away in a half-circle skid, its tires spinning and flinging dirt, and the lips encircled Yokley like lassos. Yokley rose and swung into the seat as if he were an old pro at such escapes.

His door slammed shut.

They both were joggled side to side in their seats as the truck bounced and rocked down the rutted driveway.

Mayfield held the wheel tight.

The lips guided the way on both sides — they were tracks that kept the old truck from careening out of control into the trees.

A glance at the rearview mirror showed only red dust rising behind them.

LATE THE NEXT afternoon, Yokley, Mayfield, and the lips entourage arrived in Pigeon Forge and headed toward the mountains. Mayfield and Yokley argued up the road they thought led to Catons Chapel because Mayfield wanted to find a motel and rest for the night and Yokley wanted to hurry up the mountains before dark.

Yokley was driving, so that was that.

It wasn't long before they were lost far up in the Smokies.

Mayfield said that if they found Dolly Parton's Tennessee Mountain Home it would not be open to the public, but

Yokley barnstormed right through Mayfield's interruptions and objections like in a dogfight and said he didn't care.

Just seeing the roof and satellite dish over the fence would be a goal met, Yokley said, a destination scratched off A Thousand Places to See Before Yokley Tribble Dies. If he could kick off a piece of the fence for a souvenir, even better.

The pickup jounced along a road that was only two sloping ruts and frequent hairpins through thick boxelder and moosewood trees.

Eventually the road ended at a clearing and a shack. Chickens lurched across the dirt yard. A skinny yellow pit bull was chained to a tree and barking. A Ford truck was up on cinder blocks. Two old men were playing dominos fast and loud on the rickety little front porch. They stopped and studied Mayfield and Yokley, their hands on their knees, their eyes blunt and black. One chewed slowly.

"Maybe we're here," Mayfield said. He wondered why a pit bull this far in the backwoods would be chained to a tree, but he was thankful for it because the yellow dog barked and growled and leaped, and the chain yanked him back again and again.

Mayfield got out. It was dusty and stuffy up in the mountain clearing.

Yokley waited in the truck behind the wheel. He coughed.

The lips hung behind too, hiding behind the pickup truck like scared cats.

Mayfield climbed the creaking wooden steps. It felt like déjà vu. The déjà vu evoked the dead writer's house. Crutches. Hard to believe it had happened just yesterday.

The shack's front door was open, and the inside looked

dark and large. The men were grizzly and big. The dominos were on top of an old cracker barrel between them. The barrel's hoops were rusty, and the staves were warped and gray.

A third grizzly man suddenly emerged like a shark from the shadowy front door. He aimed an ancient double-barreled shotgun at Mayfield's nose.

Quicker than a flash, the lips were a bead curtain between Mayfield and the man.

Mayfield stared up the pitted barrels and didn't know what to do. He thought the bores looked like a shark's eyes homing on him. They matched the eyes of the men.

"Get off my property," the man with the gun said.

"We're lost," Mayfield said.

Dusk was approaching. The sun would be going down. There would be no lights except their own and the fires of witch covens far off in the woods. Bears would block the road. Cross-eyed banjo players would come out from the kudzu. Their fingerboards would be axe handles, and their pegheads would be blades sharpened by moonlight.

The lips would not be able to save them this time.

"Get off my property," the man with the shotgun said again.

"What's the best way to Dolly Parton's old home place?"

"Get off my property." The man moved a few inches closer.

The cold barrels pushed aside two strands of lips and touched Mayfield's nose.

Mayfield stepped back.

The domino players rose from their straightback chairs.

Mayfield backed off the porch, his hands up—he smiled and shrugged with apology, accompanied by the lips surrounding him like a bubble—and returned backwards to Yokley's truck.

The chain rattled, the dog barked, and Mayfield hoped the man would shoot it, but the shotgun and the man's squinty-eyed aim followed his every move.

"That went well," Yokley said with his cockroach-in-the-flour look after Mayfield got in. Yokley did a wide, clumsy Y-turn that scraped his back fender on a dead, bark-stripped tree, and they left the shack behind them.

SPEED
LIMIT
55

MAYFIELD KEPT SEEING all three men's black eyes as he and Yokley slowly made their way from one winding dirt road to another until they finally came out on a paved highway curving down the mountain. He kept hearing like an earworm the story Meredith told him shortly after their wedding about the one trip she took before they met that scared her so bad she'd never go anywhere again. She told him that story only one time, but that one time was enough for Mayfield to remember every word.

Meredith started the story by showing him the picture of the Shark Lady, a middle-aged woman with deeply tanned skin and sun-bleached, wind-blown hair—

she ran a shark diving business for adventurous tourists

told me if you get stung three times by a scorpion you drop dead on the spot

get bit three times by a shark and you might live

she lowered her cage in the water, I got in, and down I went through a cloud of chum so thick and red you couldn't find your hand in front of your face

when the water clears and you see that great white coming at you rolling on his side with his mouth open, you wonder if the rusty bars of the cage will hold

(young newlywed Meredith paused here and put her picture back in the envelope)

then maybe you wish that they won't—

Many times over the years, Mayfield tried to imagine himself on such a reckless dive with Meredith. He wondered what he'd do if the bars broke and a shark got at them. Supposing Meredith was hit first, would Mayfield try to help them get away? Or would fear slash through him like the shark's teeth, make him leave Meredith and swim like mad for the surface?

Something about that Shark Lady's picture, Mayfield thought. He never saw it again after Meredith told him that story only once.

It was getting late, and the light was fading. Mayfield told Yokley to just forget about Dolly Parton.

YOKLEY TOOK A wrong turn the next morning after they crossed the Smokies to Cherokee, and they ended up in Maggie Valley. Yokley said he was hungry and wanted to stop. He pulled the truck off the highway in the shade of a mountain by a diner with an empty dirt parking lot.

The diner had no name, just DINER on the sign. It was a

trailer with pink curtains. The diner was dark and narrow inside. Three card tables and folding chairs were set up in the front room. A black and white Shih Tzu with long, tangled hair yipped at them when they entered.

Mayfield and Yokley sat down.

The Shih Tzu followed, lay down, and panted next to the table.

A counter separated the kitchen from the tables. The only people other than Yokley and Mayfield were a short-order cook in a greasy apron and a heavy waitress with an exhausted pine-nut face who shook the diner when she walked. Her hair was wrapped in a red handkerchief.

"The only thing missing here," Yokley said, "is the nickelodeon."

Above the counter, the lips formed a Ferris wheel that turned slowly.

Before Mayfield could ask Yokley what he meant by nickelodeon, the short-order cook said from the kitchen, "Dog's name is Houston."

The dog stared at the Ferris wheel above the counter. Mayfield was intrigued. Maybe it meant he wasn't imagining the lips after all.

"What can I get you folks?" the waitress said. She looked at Yokley. She looked at Mayfield.

This morning, Mayfield had woken up wanting to ditch Yokley somewhere. The past couple days, he'd been embarrassed when waitresses assumed they were together as if Mayfield couldn't do better, so, to shoot down assumptions, he would say right away to split the check.

No one ever asked outright if they were together, but

Mayfield saw it in their eyes. Some offered a glimmer of condescending approval. Others squinted with veiled contempt. Mayfield even asked Yokley to wait in the truck while checking into their cheap motels, which Yokley was happy to do.

Mayfield was hesitant to give this waitress in Maggie Valley the benefit of the doubt, but he did — the waitress was *not* assuming he and Yokley were together, and he did *not* have to hurry up and say separate checks.

"Menus," Yokley said.

"I saw that same red handkerchief," Mayfield said, pointing to the waitress' head, "in a painting."

The waitress made a cooing sound that rose at the end like a question and tucked some silver hair under the handkerchief. "Well, ain't got no menus," she said. "Specials today are biscuits and gravy or scrambled eggs and bacon." She pointed to the whiteboard by the door, where the two specials were written with choppy red letters and misspelled words.

"No grits?" Mayfield said.

"Not this morning, no. Fresh on Monday."

"Bring one of each," Yokley said. "We'll share."

The dog continued staring at the Ferris wheel above the counter.

The waitress brought the food to them and collapsed at the next table while they ate.

The short-order cook, an old man of about seventy, came from around the counter and sat at the third table. His white beard and mustache were stained yellow around his mouth. He lit a cigarette.

Yokley closed his eyes, waved some air toward his face, and inhaled deeply.

The waitress sighed and yawned.

"Where you from?" the cook said.

"Georgia," Yokley said.

Mayfield cut his biscuit in half and slid it with some gravy onto Yokley's plate. He took one of the bacon strips and a forkful of eggs off Yokley's.

Yokley attacked his food and gulped it all down in only a few bites. He scraped up the gravy with his spoon.

"Golly," the waitress said, "I forgot if you wanted coffee or something."

"Black," Yokley said.

"Sugar and cream," Mayfield said.

She pulled herself to her feet and limped toward the kitchen. "Hips," she said. "Oh, they hurt."

"Got any children?" the short order cook said to Mayfield and Yokley.

Mayfield and Yokley both said no.

The waitress brought two cups of coffee and sat back down expelling another sigh and moan. "Children," she said. "Darla Sue's son, Bobby Daryl, only stops by to see his mama when his truck breaks down again and he needs money to fix it. And that wife of his is homemade ugly."

"If it's got tits or tires, he's going to have trouble with it," the cook said.

"Language," the waitress said.

"But she can sure pull a vacuum on an onion sack," the cook said and laughed at himself.

Mayfield ate the last bite of bacon and left most of his

biscuit on his plate. Yokley speared it with his fork and swallowed it all at once.

"Mind your manners," the waitress said.

Mayfield didn't know if she was talking to the cook or to Yokley.

"Bad manners are better than no manners at all," the cook said.

Yokley shot the cook a flash of recognition, laughed, and said to him, "That's the trouble with the world today — nobody reads anymore."

"What's that got to do with the price of tea in China?" the waitress said after raising her hands and putting them back down.

Mayfield didn't understand either. A long silence stretched over the table as he and Yokley finished their coffee and the cook crushed his cigarette butt on a saucer.

"So." The waitress looked at Mayfield and Yokley. "What kind of work you gentlemen do?"

Mayfield rarely welcomed this question even in retirement. He never wanted to answer it truthfully. He was embarrassed to say he spent his life in a greenhouse, and the question reminded him how much he'd hated it, reminded him he dressed up when he was off work to make people think he was more successful than he was.

"Antiques," Yokley said.

"Art," Mayfield said.

The Shih Tzu next to the table panted louder. It hadn't stopped staring at the Ferris wheel above the counter.

"Butter me up and call me a biscuit," the waitress said, and Mayfield wondered if she talked like that all the time.

They paid and got up to leave.

The cook wiped the counter. "You fellows going to be in town a while?" he said, his arm circling the towel over the shiny countertop. "Tonight there's a pig chase at the football field. Fireworks too."

The lips streaked in a single line to the ceiling, flared in several directions, trailed down to the floor.

"Awfully dry for fireworks," Yokley said.

"Darla Sue is inviting everybody over for a greased watermelon party in her pool," the waitress said.

The lips hung. All made puzzled expressions as if scratching their heads.

They were swept aside like a curtain for a lean and lithe delivery man hefting in a cumbersome box.

"It's here!" said the waitress, her face aglow in excitement.

The delivery man handed the box off to the cook by setting it on the counter and sliding it into the cook's arms.

The cook grunted, steadied himself, and hauled it into the kitchen.

"One more," the delivery man announced. He strode out the door.

The waitress hobbled after the cook, and a few seconds later the sounds of lifting, dropping, and scraping came from somewhere back beyond the kitchen.

The delivery man returned with another box, set it on the counter with some effort, muscles rippling under his shirt, nodded to Mayfield, nodded to Yokley, and left once more.

Mayfield and Yokley both regarded the box, met eyes, and silently told each other the same thing:

Let's take it.

The box weighed about thirty-five pounds, but the two of them were able to maneuver it together fleetly. The Shih Tzu followed them to the door. Mayfield propped his side of the box on his hip and bent down to scratch the dog's ears.

It kept its eyes on the lips circling above Mayfield.

The delivery truck was pulling away and accelerating down the highway toward a curve up a hill. Mayfield felt assured the driver had no idea they'd swiped the package.

Yokley let the tailgate fall, and Mayfield slid the box down the truck bed. Yokley bent down, his hands on his knees, and coughed some.

Off they went when he was done. Both exhaled in relief at the clean getaway. Yokley let out a few small coughs, and he was breathing easily again.

A hundred miles later, Mayfield couldn't help picturing watermelons popping up from shiny, bare arms that were grabbing and squeezing and bare chests that were splashing water rainbows.

SPEED
LIMIT
55

A CEMETERY THAT hadn't buried anyone in a century was where Yokley stopped the truck to inspect the box and find out what was inside. The cemetery had gone unmaintained for years—the grass that had been allowed to grow untended was now fallen yellow and brown around the leaning headstones. The letters on all the stones were blurred to illegibility.

A sign informed them they were ten miles from Big Stone

Gap.

The box was on the dropped tailgate. The lips were observing from up high.

"Sent from the Czech Republic," Mayfield said, reading the label.

Yokley sliced the taped-down corner with his thumbnail and pried the flaps apart.

Twelve bottles, necks up. An image of gun bores flashed through Mayfield's mind while registering that the box contained bottles.

Yokley pulled one out, traced the label with the same thumb he used to break the tape.

"Green fairy," he said and grinned yellow like he'd struck gold or hit a jackpot.

Mayfield took the bottle and traced the label too.

ABSENTA in red old-world letters over a sugar skull.

He'd never heard of it.

"We're on a leave of absinthe," Yokley said.

SPEED
LIMIT
55

THEIR NEXT STOP was the Fitzgerald House in Montgomery. Zelda's *Mad Tea Party* painting was Yokley's objective, but Mayfield failed to distract the pimply college-kid volunteer long enough for Yokley to snatch it and dash to the truck undiscovered, and Yokley started coughing anyway. They left empty handed.

They discussed the need to plan more carefully.

Mayfield wanted to see Hank Williams' grave. They stopped there on the way out of town. Before the absinthe,

Mayfield had never had a drop to drink in his life, but buying an airline-size bottle of bourbon from a package store to splash a few drops on the Astroturf around Luke the Drifter's granite hat had felt like the right thing to do.

He swore he heard "the silence of a falling star" warbling through the trees at sundown.

Yokley said, "I don't know where I'd put the *Tea Party* anyway."

SPEED
LIMIT
55

A CHEAP MOTEL for the night.

Mayfield brought up Hank Williams' grave and asked Yokley if he thought it was true that Hank's real hat had been cast in granite like bronzed baby shoes. "If so," Mayfield said, "I wish there was a way to break it off the tombstone."

Yokley set out sugar cubes and two slotted spoons. He poured two glasses of absinthe.

Mayfield watched the milky spirals weave. He saw in them the white and vapory brim of Hank's hat.

Soon Yokley poured a second glass of absinthe for himself and turned the light off without touching it. His whistling and wheezing snores lilted like a sagging balloon from his bed on the other side of the room.

Mayfield slowly sipped his way through his glass of absinthe. He left Yokley's. He lay awake for a long time. When he finally fell asleep, the shotgun bores in his dreams had blinking blue eyes and long eye lashes.

SPEED
LIMIT
55

he wasn't going to let her bring the chandelier home but had relented when she told him it most certainly would fit in their living room and, besides, it would be free, so they borrowed yokley's truck to haul it away from the hotel that was about to be torn down on the other side of town, and when they got there the chandelier was sitting in the front carhop looking carelessly rejected with its strands of diamond-shaped crystals splayed out under its weight and its narrow upper structure lopsided like a bent flagpole

they lugged the chandelier home as carefully as they could so as not to break any part of it — the bottom round part of the chandelier was about ten feet wide, and all together the whole chandelier was about eight feet high, weighed 200 pounds, mayfield guessed

mayfield and meredith managed to collapse it somewhat and bundle it together to get it tilted sideways through the front door of their house — when they pushed all the furniture against the walls and finished hoisting the monstrous thing with a chain threaded up to the attic through a hole drilled in the ceiling, meredith smiled and clasped her hands by her throat

SPEED
LIMIT
55

IN THE MORNING, Mayfield dealt with the annoyance of a steamy bathroom that lacked a fan vent. He hated steamy bathrooms without fans. He waved a howling hairdryer over the fogged mirror until his face, tired and haggard, emerged in clear detail and ruddy color.

The lips bordered the mirror like a vanity and gave the steam a reddish, hell-like glow.

He remembered when the eyes in his reflection were fuller, the skin smoother, and now in his cheeks and chin he saw folds and shades of his father and grandfather rising like submarines.

SPEED
LIMIT
55

IN MEMPHIS, THEY lounged by the indoor pool at the Peabody a few days and ventured out in the heat only twice. They spun under the influence of absinthe, toured Sun Studio, and ate barbeque in a blues joint on Beale Street, where Yokley licked his fingers and ordered a second plate of pulled pork.

The lips probably went with them. They were like floaters in Mayfield's eyes now — he didn't notice them until he tried looking right at them, and when he did they zipped from his vision, and his eyes hurt when they tried keeping up.

It never occurred to Mayfield to suggest Graceland until they were just outside Carbondale. Yokley said there was no chance of turning back. Mayfield stewed and wished he could drive again.

SPEED
LIMIT
55

THE FARTHER NORTH they drove, the hotter it got and the more Yokley coughed. When the landscape flattened, the ground was dead and brown and crumbly as far as Mayfield could see.

All they had to show for a thousand miles on the road was a pair of old crutches in the truck bed and eight bottles of absinthe packed in a shipping box from the Czech Republic.

They pushed on. Somewhere in middle Illinois, they rolled into a small town that lacked a sign boasting a name.

A rusty lawnmower sat in a half-mowed yard. The yard was shaved and tamped down where it had been mowed but overgrown with parched, dead grass higher than the mower's wheels where it hadn't been.

A door leaned on a tree that had lost all its limbs. A faded holiday wreath hung on the door.

Several old TVs stacked three high hid every inch of concrete in front of a garage. The windows were busted out, and the door had fallen off its tracks. The garage squatted next to an empty foundation.

They approached the town center, and Yokley pointed to a brick storefront up the block. The sign above the window advertised the storefront as a chocolate museum.

Mayfield's interest piqued.

But it turned out to be so hot inside he almost stepped back out. Which would have been just as well because the place was empty except for a folding chair and a desk with a cash box.

A tall, thin young man who looked about seventeen years of age and wearing a dirty apron emerged from a back room fanning himself with a folded sheet of paper. "The chocolate is melting," he said. His face was pinched in panic, and his voice was high and shaky. "The air conditioning stopped working a few hours ago," he said, "and I don't know what do about the sculpture."

Mayfield was primed to rush out of there without looking back, but Yokley started a conversation with the young man.

"Sculpture?" Yokley said.

"Please help me," the young man said.

He led them into the back room.

A four-funneled ocean liner six feet long and nearly a foot wide sat on a narrow table barely sturdy enough to support it. The liner's portholes, rivets, steel plates, and superstructure were detailed but somewhat hazily defined.

Recognition hit Mayfield. Chocolate. A ship made out of chocolate. And its details were softening in the heat.

"It's the *Titanic*," Yokley said, his tree-for-the-first-time expression spreading from eyes to mouth.

A pair of lips popped into focus and perched on the crow's nest. A few more followed and settled on the rigging like birds on a wire.

"I don't know," Mayfield said, "if there is anything we can do about this."

"It's melting," the young man said. He rubbed his hands up and down his apron, which Mayfield now realized was blotched with melted chocolate.

"I see fingerprints there," Yokley said. He pointed to an area on the bow where smudges circled across several portholes and smushed them in.

"I tried to fix it," the young man said. "Please. What do I do?"

Yokley shrugged.

"It's melting," the young man said again.

"It's an impressive sculpture," Yokley said. "Not technically accurate, but impressive."

Mayfield wished he knew as much about something as Yokley knew about everything. "I don't think you can ask for more out of chocolate," Mayfield said.

"Sorry," Yokley said. "I was being selfish."

Mayfield said, "I imagine *Titanic* enthusiasts such as yourself have pointed out the inaccuracies."

"We can be assholes like that," Yokley said.

"Will you please help me?" the young man said. "It's melting. Melting." Fear was shivering in his voice now, and he was fondling his elbows with his arms crossed.

Using both hands, Yokley broke off the first funnel.

The young man sucked in his breath.

The chocolate funnel was too big to fit in his mouth, so Yokley, his palms smeared, took a bite from the soft corner.

The young man bugged his eyes.

"And the melting chocolate, I must say, is a tad bitter," Yokley said, his mouth full. He offered the rest of the first funnel to the young man, who recoiled as if Yokley were showing him a copperhead.

"Now you have another inaccuracy," Mayfield said, "for, you see, *Titanic* had four smokestacks, and at present your chocolate sculpture only has three." Mayfield held up three fingers. He didn't know much about the *Titanic*, but he knew it had four smokestacks, and this boosted his confidence in announcing so.

"Oh, I say," Yokley cried, "how careless of you!" He hopped forward, thrust the chocolate stack at the young man, and waved it back and forth like a rapier.

The young man was crying now and clearly had had enough. He pulled off his apron, threw it on the floor, and charged from the room. The front door squeaked open and slammed shut—its bell tinkled hard.

"Are we taking this?" Mayfield said.

Yokley bit off another piece, chewed, swallowed, and said, "No — it'll melt all over the truck."

And Mayfield was embarrassed he'd asked.

SPEED
LIMIT
55

MAYFIELD FELT TOO much of the trip was wasted on mundane aspects of traveling such as dividing a duffel with an imaginary line so that dirty clothes didn't mix with clean. Did last week's boxers go rolled on the bottom, clean ones flat on top? Yellow-collared shirts on the left, fresh on the right? Mayfield could never decide.

Another cheap motel.

The air conditioner rattled, clicked, and clacked. Yokley was out shopping for eucalyptus oil. He'd promised to bring back burgers and fries and shakes.

Mayfield was bored. The television was fuzzy and buzzed static. For something to do, Mayfield tried turning on the closed captioning, but he ended up throwing the remote control at the flatscreen in frustration.

He opened and closed empty drawers. In the nightstand next to the Gideon Bible, he found an unopened shoe polish can. He turned it over and read the back, wanting to know who had left it and why. How long it had been there. If anyone else who'd stayed in the room had found it.

He couldn't remember the last time he'd seen a shoe polish can.

Screeching violins, violas, and cellos burst from the fuzzy television. Mayfield started. His heart quickened. His throat tightened.

And here he was in a cheap motel in the middle of nowhere.

He laughed lightly to himself and shook his head. An idea for a scare came to him. Yokley deserved one.

At first, Mayfield had been lukewarm about the trip. He grew excited, however, in the hundred miles or so before Andalusia, but Andalusia showed him how unprepared Yokley was.

What was Yokley's plan for the earrings and shoes? Was he going to throw a towel over a crutch, hold the crutch like a shotgun, barge in, and take them?

The obvious answer was to knock on the door and ask nicely.

But even that was strange. Who did that? Who showed up at a return address and said, "Excuse me, I'm sorry to bother you, but you didn't send me the shoes and earrings"?

can you tell me how to get to dolly parton's old home place

Mayfield wasn't confident Yokley had thought anything through, and all they had as a result was a pair of old crutches and a box of absinthe.

Seven bottles, the last he'd counted.

Mayfield was going to scare the dumb fuck, if only for something to do.

He took down the shower curtain, spread it on his bed, and got to work with the shoe polish.

The lips provided a pattern to trace. Mayfield sketched the pattern first with a pencil eraser dipped in shoe polish. The lips backed away and watched from above, chittering like school kids.

Mayfield filled in the pattern with an old sock.

He let the curtain dry fifteen minutes or so and carefully dragged it back to the bathroom. Biting his lip, he snapped each shower curtain ring shut and spread the curtain fully open.

He wiped sweat off his forehead. The air conditioner was old. The room wasn't as cool as it should have been, and the bathroom got no cool air at all.

But the curtain was a masterpiece, Mayfield thought.

A silhouette of an old lady in a dress. Hair back and in a bun. Arm up, knife in her hand.

Yokley didn't wear his glasses in the shower, so he'd see it only as a vague shadow, not a crude shoe polish design.

Maybe it would scare the breath out of him.

He slid the curtain along the rod until it came together in a vertical bundle next to the tile. The shoe polish silhouette was a column of indistinguishable black blobs this way.

His sight being so bad, Yokley would probably mistake them for tropical fish. Until he pulled the shower curtain shut.

ha! ha!

What was that story Yokley was talking about the other day? Something about "a tub had caught all—ha! ha!"?

Mayfield turned off the bathroom light and threw away the sock and shoe polish can.

The prank turned out to be a dud, though, which was sorely disappointing to Mayfield. Yokley came back with two bags of food and two shakes in a paper carrier. He ate sitting on his bed. Mayfield ate standing up.

Mayfield reached the bottom of his cup, and his straw

made sucking noises.

Was he going to take a shower or not?

Yokley scrunched up the two bags, threw them in the trash, and poured two glasses of absinthe.

Sugar cubes. Slotted spoons.

Well?

But before the night was dark, Yokley was already asleep, tossing and turning in a wheezy dream.

At sunrise, he told Mayfield to hurry up and shower. Time to hit the road.

Mayfield watched the water wash the shoe polish off the curtain. The polish swirled down the drain like chocolate sauce.

SPEED
LIMIT
55

THE AFTERNOONS FLOATED in absinthe clouds and ruby sparkles in his peripheral vision. His thoughts wound around what would happen to his nerves and blood vessels in his belly if he lost weight. Would the nerves and blood vessels shrink and disappear with the fat cells, or would they stay behind and leave a tangled ball compressing the lungs and liver? Most afternoons riding around, there was nothing else to do but think. Mayfield's green, pooling brain was full of philosophy wispy like fog on a morning lake.

This particular afternoon, however, Mayfield's brain was clear because Yokley was feeling under the weather after a long coughing spell, and Mayfield was behind the wheel again for once. They'd pulled over for lunch. Mayfield tossed his sandwich wrapper out the window, propped his arms on the steering wheel, and stared out the windshield.

Heat waves shimmered in the distance beyond the dry field where he'd parked to eat. A small dust devil twirled off to the right about a mile away, but a wind puff soon erased it. He couldn't quite recall how many motels the two of them had slept in or how many towns they'd been through in the past week. The transit days were blurry in his mind. Surreal suspensions of rhythm, he thought. Snappy connections between one day of familiarity in the pickup to another.

"But don't marriages just fall apart sometimes?" Yokley said. "Like a jar of marbles when you drop it?" Yokley's feet were up on a small cooler in the footwell. He had no shirt on. He'd left his coat behind in a motel the other morning. His pale skin glistened, his hair was damp over his ears, and his fern-green jogging pants were cut into frayed shorts now. Sweat was dripping down his glasses.

Half-dressed like that, he was bony and lanky like a marionette.

After some silence, Yokley added, "Let me tell you something interesting—I read an article last winter about all the people who tried going over Niagara Falls in a barrel."

That might have sounded adventurous to Mayfield if Yokley had told him about it before this trip. The one lesson Mayfield learned better than any other? That travel and adventure were only glamorous to those who had never traveled. There always comes a journey too, he thought, when a frequent traveler will not reach his destination.

"Your truck's air conditioner sure picked a hell of good time to break down," Mayfield said.

"I need a shower," Yokley said.

"We can make it home by tomorrow morning if we drive straight through all night."

Yokley didn't reply for a long time. The silence made Mayfield want to fidget and start small talk about something else, but he looked over his shoulder through the cab's back window. The duffel bags were still there. The one full of paperbacks was unzipped, and some of the books, their covers missing, were poking out. The absinthe box was still there too. So were the crutches.

Of course they were still there, Mayfield thought. They couldn't just get up and fly away.

Yokley broke the quiet. "We have to pick up the shoes and earrings."

Mayfield fiddled with the windshield wiper lever. "Which way should we go?" he said.

"West."

"Out of Cedar Falls or Des Moines?"

"Cedar Falls," Yokley said. "Stay off the Interstate."

Mayfield opened a map. The folds in the yellow paper had ripped, and different sections of Iowa buckled in his lap. A hot breeze drifted in and rattled the ragged edges. Mayfield started to fold a corner down, scrunched up the map instead, and tossed it out the window. It blew down the road, bouncing and spinning. "Let's go," he said.

Yokley said, "Don't you need the map?"

"You know the way."

Yokley shrugged. "Just keep going west on the back roads. When we get to Nebraska, keep heading west."

"Valentine by seven then?" Mayfield said. He started the truck and pulled onto the highway. No other cars were around. They overtook the map, which was still skipping down the shoulder.

Yokley leaned out the window and tried to catch it, but it was just beyond his reach.

Mayfield adjusted the rearview mirror and watched the map disappear behind them. He considered going back to get it, but he only angled the mirror down so that the crutches and absinthe box reflected in it. He kept one eye on the road and one eye on the mirror.

Mayfield readjusted the mirror and shifted his full attention back to the road. "Wonder when this heat'll start to let up," he said.

Yokley stuck his arm out the window and waved his hand around in the rushing wind. "You know what it feels like when you stick your hand out the window?"

"What?"

"Like when you lean over the side of a boat and trail it in cool ocean water."

shark lady

The two men continued riding for about an hour without saying anything. Every once in a while, Mayfield passed a slow semi. The flat Iowa countryside slipped on by as the intensity of early midday melted into the sluggish surrealism of late afternoon. They passed through two small towns whose names Mayfield forgot as soon as they blew past the last gas station and empty Chinese buffet.

"How's the gas?" Yokley said.

"Enough left for a hundred miles or so."

After about another hour driving in silence, they crossed into Nebraska. Twenty miles past the state line, Yokley told

Mayfield to keep west on a different isolated country road. The Nebraska landscape was just as flat as Iowa had been, and the road unwound before them perfectly straight into the burnt-sienna drought dust.

Before long, it seemed the weather had changed somewhat since they left Iowa. The heat became heavier and stickier. The breeze was gone. Mayfield felt a little uncomfortable, as if he couldn't get enough air. He had a strange feeling that it had become just a little darker outside, but the sun still shone. The sky was clear except for a band of grayish-white froth piling up in the distance above the horizon. He couldn't be sure because of the air rushing past the open windows, but Mayfield thought he heard, or at least felt, the faint grumbling of far-off thunder.

Yokley pointed. "Looks like a storm up ahead."

"It hasn't rained since the beginning of April."

"Keep going toward it," Yokley said. "The end is in sight."

The end is in sight, Mayfield echoed in his mind.

The truck had begun to drift over the center line. Mayfield shifted the steering wheel a little until it was back in the middle.

Another half hour of silence passed before they approached an eighteen-wheeler parked on the side of the highway about a mile ahead. Like the clouds in the sky, it grew larger as they approached it.

The pickup rattled over a spine-jarring bump. The back end bounced up and lurched back down. The crutches and absinthe bottles rattled in the bed. Mayfield checked behind him. The tailgate hadn't swung open, so he kept driving.

A strange smell crept into the cab. At first, Mayfield

thought it smelled like the inside of a dirty wayside on a hot day. It also smelled like fertilizer. Like the inside of the delivery truck at the greenhouse outside of town where he had worked most his life and marriage.

The strange smell was growing stronger. Stranger. Death-like.

The eighteen-wheeler was only a few hundred feet ahead now, and Mayfield guessed that was where the smell was coming from. The flatbed trailer was piled full of cows. Their legs, coated with dried, flaky manure, stuck out between the gaps in the trailer's barred enclosure.

All at once, the stench became overpowering.

Mayfield gagged, covered his nose, fought against his stomach twisting.

Yokley cleared his throat, coughed forcefully three times, and pushed up his glasses.

"Those must be some of the cows that died in the heat," Yokley said, "the ones the guy on the news was talking about."

Cough, cough, cough.

Several bovine heads hung over the top of the flatbed's enclosure. Their eyes were open and lifeless, and their tongues lolled from wide-open mouths.

Yokley coughed again and leaned out the window. The wind blew his hair. He pulled himself back in the cab. "The driver was in the ditch puking," he said.

Mayfield slammed his fist against the steering wheel. "This is nuts."

The truck swerved a little to the right and grazed the shoulder.

Mayfield yanked the wheel to the left and the truck rolled back onto the pavement. He clenched his jaw and fought to ignore the smell, which, to his relief, was growing fainter as they rode down the highway away from the cow truck.

The storm was swelling fast before them.

A few raindrops splattered on the windshield. Now the sky hummed green. Lightning flickered subtly within the threatening clouds swirling just ahead. A long bolt careened from another cloud about a mile away. After about five seconds, Mayfield was sure he heard the thunder that time.

The two men in the pickup pushed on down the highway into the storm.

A clean, showery smell washed away the lingering traces of heat decay following them. They crossed the boundary between light and dark, where the clear sky dissolved in a gloriously wicked mess and the shadows underneath the low-hanging clouds drove out the last stubborn rays of sun. The darkness rushed in over the highway behind the pickup as if to seal off the only route back to the light. A cold wind gust blasted into the open windows.

A water sheet smacked the windshield and melted away the road.

Mayfield flipped on the wipers and rolled up his window.

Lightning exploded all around the pickup in a savage tantrum as tiny ice grains pelted the windshield. They were so light they rode in the water rivers that shimmied up the glass in defiance of the wipers.

Larger ice pieces began falling. First, they were about the size of peas. They grew to the size of shooter marbles. They drummed the roof and cracked the windshield.

sometimes it's like a jar of marbles when you drop it

Mayfield slowed to a crawl. The wind rocked the truck and sent water and ice flying everywhere. Lightning popped like flashbulbs in a dark closet.

Yokley's window was still open. He was drenched, and he was smiling yellow again. Small hailstones were stuck in his hair like sequins on a veil.

"Some storm," Mayfield said. He wanted to tell Yokley to roll up his window, but something kept him from saying it.

The rain and hail all of a sudden stopped, and the wind became hot and sticky.

"Looks like it might be at the most an F3," Yokley said.

Mayfield saw what had Yokley's attention.

The gray tentacle emerging from the swirling clouds about a mile ahead over the highway spun like whirling cotton candy as lightning sparkled around it. It extended down toward the ground and pulled back up.

It reached for the ground again—dirt and debris flew up in a twirling surge to darken the funnel more. After it made contact with the earth, the tornado swelled and weaved on a course for the pickup.

Mayfield hit the brakes. They suddenly softened like a sponge. He wrenched the wheel to the left until the pickup swung into a fast skid.

The pickup left the highway and nosed down the ditch. A bang and a shudder, and it kicked up dirt and rattled up the other side.

"We're too close," Yokley said, pressing the ceiling with both hands.

Uneasiness rose up and tightened Mayfield's throat.

Mayfield whirled the wheel back, but the truck slid sideways, the passenger side facing the approaching tornado, until it scraped to a stop.

Mayfield kept his hands on the wheel. His arms ached, his tooth throbbed, and his fear mushroomed in him.

SPEED
LIMIT
55

a plunge in the chilly autumn water behind their house – he hardly ever paid attention to meredith's night wanderings as long as she didn't leave the house, only this time she did and he didn't catch her – and he went looking for her and found her floating faceup only twenty feet from the dock where he tied up his rowboat in summer

mockernut hickory leaf in her hair, one oar that she'd hauled out from the garage floating next to her, splattered triangle of blood shining on the dock's sharp, splintery corner where she'd slipped and hit her head

SPEED
LIMIT
55

THE WIND BELLOWED into the cab and shook the truck.

"There's a tornado," Mayfield said.

"When it's coming right at you, you don't just...sit there." Yokley shoved the door open and stepped out in the storm. The wind propelled him against the truck, but Yokley pushed his way toward the truck's rear.

The truck rocked more roughly as the tornado slithered closer. It was now only about three-quarters of a mile away and bearing down fast.

"Where are you going?" Mayfield forced open his door and jumped out too. The wind knocked the breath out of him, and he stumbled and fell to the ground. Dust and grit stung his eyes, and pebbles jabbed his skin. He scrambled up and trudged toward the rear too. He held the gunwales tightly.

Yokley was opposite him, also holding the gunwales tightly. He leaned against the wind and faced the tornado, which was now only about a half mile away. His hair whipped straight back.

"Let's go," Mayfield yelled. He shielded his face with his arm and looked up at the tornado. It loomed only a thousand feet away. His skin was stinging all over from the flying dirt and pebbles.

SPEED LIMIT
55

water so calm and smooth and clear while he pulled her body in over slippery rocks that a million moon faces and fish faces and meredith faces grinned howled snickered frowned jeered at him, faces that were just under the surface yet a thousand miles under

SPEED LIMIT
55

YOKLEY DIDN'T MOVE.

Mayfield wondered what he must look like to Yokley, and he recognized that Yokley was just as alone as he was. He'd lived next door for years, but Mayfield knew only that Yokley ambled around town, his belt tailing him from a single belt loop. That he'd started spending his pensions on memorabilia. That he spent just as much on glass cases and dehumidifiers to protect it. That lately he'd started stealing what he could. This was the only secret Mayfield remembered Yokley sharing with him in all the years they were neighbors.

A dehumidifier had broken and launched Yokley into a panic about mildew. Mayfield had met Yokley in the granny flat and examined it. It was next to a display case. Three smiling mannequins inside wore faded TV show dresses. Mayfield turned the dehumidifier around and looked at the back panel.

While he was unscrewing it, Yokley showed him a yellowed and crinkly napkin with smudged lipstick on it.

"Her lipstick", boasted Yokley, "from her very lips." Yokley went on to explain that the napkin was taken out of the trash in the CBS commissary by a custodian who used to stalk her. It was right around the time she taped Yokley's favorite episode, "The Little Dictator."

"And now I own it," Yokley said. "Highest bidder."

Bang, there it was. The first pair of lips.

It floated in the corner of Mayfield's eye. Followed him out the granny flat, across Yokley's yard—he swatted at the thing *a speck? a hair? a bug?* while walking—across his own yard, into his own house, where it multiplied without him knowing how. All he did was sit down on the olive couch in front of the chandelier, blink, and they were all just there.

Late that night, Mayfield turned the TV on and there, smiling through the cranberry chandelier that reflected prisms from the sterile streetlight coming through the new windows, was a set of lips, big and bright and red, singing a song about picture shows.

Mayfield turned the TV off right away and went to bed. He put his pajamas on in the glowing-dark bedroom and tried not to look at the lump the pillow made on the other side of the bed, the lump that he still sometimes thought was Meredith waiting for him.

—flying kisses in the dark

He turned over on his other side, pulled the covers up under his chin, and shut his eyes tight against the red glow from the lips.

—who's leading me on here?

In the middle of the night, Mayfield yanked the pillow away from his eyes.

They were all still there, hundreds of little lips fluttering around and around, leaving those bright trails. Mayfield supposed he should try counting sheep, and maybe the lips would go away. Of course he tried counting the lips first. That didn't work.

—what's leading me on here?

Nor did it work the next night, and the night after that. And by departure morning, the check still hadn't cleared, and the same operator hung up on him.

—why?

Yokley's nose, forehead, and bald spot were a butt-slapped red. He'd refused sunscreen the whole trip. His cheeks were puffy, and his eyes bulged through thick lids behind thick lenses.

His face had quickly turned pale and sweaty. His lips had shadowed to a bluish-purple tint.

Mayfield couldn't breathe well either. He choked on the

rushing air. He held his breath two minutes underwater the last time he swam in the lake before Meredith died, but this must be what asthma pythons constricting around airways, or a heart lurching to a stop while blood clawed for oxygen, felt like. His strength was almost gone, and he wasn't sure how much longer he could stand. He stopped thinking of his fear slashing through him like shark's teeth —

leave Meredith and swim like mad for the surface

—how much time did he have to save himself if he left Yokley behind?

rusty bars will hold

then maybe you wish they won't

Yokley's arms and purple hands went slack at his sides, and his face, icy and blue, turned up to the scouring-pad sky his open-mouth, tree-studying expression, only his eyes were shut.

then maybe you wish they won't?

Yokley's mouth moved in the patterns of words, but no sound came. He choked. His chest convulsed. His cheeks puffed and flattened, and he spat out a cloud of cranberry glass shards.

The wind propelled the shards in a high-speed half circle across the field. A few nicked Mayfield's face and arms and drew blood like shaving cuts.

Lips sprouted out Yokley's mouth like feathers. They straightened to a long line that came out and out and out. They looped and clustered in the air between Yokley and Mayfield and fluttered skyward and faded, but more lips replaced them, and soon they circled Yokley from head to toe so fast that Yokley was enveloped in a red cloud.

One mouth broke from the rest and hovered before Yokley's lips. The mouth waited a moment—on your mark, get set—and then zipped—GO!—toward Yokley's mouth and pressed tight as if superglue were setting between them. The disembodied lips squeezed and pulled at Yokley's lips, giving mouth-to-mouth while a second set of lips suddenly joined in and hammered Yokley's chest.

The strangest thing was the surge of rancor rising from the depths of Mayfield's subconsciousness like a torpedoing great white. With this surge came the unexpected taste of pokeberries, and Mayfield somehow knew Yokley was tasting it too at that same moment.

The taste was associated with a Meredith of a long, long time ago, almost forgotten, before marriage-worn Meredith took up shop in Mayfield's memory filmstrip of the past few decades. She was nineteen when they met. Mayfield twenty. Her father still forbade her from having make-up, and the first time Mayfield and Meredith went on a date she snuck to her backyard and rubbed pokeberries on her lips.

For the first time in years and years, Mayfield tasted that first-kiss pokeberry bitterness.

Yokley leaned back, wavered a moment as if the laws of physics didn't know which way to push him, and pivoted so he was prone and hovering above the gunwale.

The red cloud enveloping Yokley exploded like a supernova. Mayfield ducked, and all the lips whipped through his hair. He kept his eyes open to watch—there was no way he could look away now.

The lips shot single file toward the tornado and looped and looped and looped a series of half hitch knots—

"Two wraps and a hooey," Mayfield said to himself
—from tip to cloud, and the tornado stopped a moment,
pulsing red like a beating heart.

The wind was flashfrozen too.

Mayfield's eyes were locked on the sight. Somewhere in
the pulsing, between half hitch knots high above, Yokley's
mouth was still sprouting feather lips and broken cranberry
glass, but it was like Yokley was on the other side of a mirror,
and the lips and glass from his mouth flew nowhere.

A blink and the lips were gone, and the wind was roaring,
and the tornado was bearing down again.

Instinct took over, and Mayfield was just Mayfield again.
Greenhouse Mayfield. Meredith's husband Mayfield.
Mayfield who never thought about anything. No rubbish
philosophy. Mayfield had no time to think anyway. All he
could do was fight against the tempest, climb in the cab, and
pull his door shut.

A large stone, about the size of a baseball, smacked the
windshield and left a sprawling spiderweb pattern on the
glass.

Mayfield floored the gas and used one hand to swing the
wheel hard to the left. With the other, he pulled his seatbelt
on. He straightened the steering wheel when he was sure he
was driving away from the tornado.

The truck tore across the field toward the highway. It
clattered down the ditch and flew up the other side. The
highway passed underneath it, and the wheels spun in
empty air. The wind caught the back end and lifted it up
until the ground filled the windshield. The cooler spilled its
ice and cans.

The truck nose rose up and swung in mid-air back toward the highway. Mayfield shoved the wheel to the right, to the left, but nothing happened.

The truck suddenly stabilized and dropped to the ground. Spinning tires pounded on the pavement and caught with a squeal.

Mayfield centered the steering wheel as the truck lurched forward. It continued to rock and twist in the wind, but he managed to stay on a straight course down the center line.

The dead cows fell from the sky. Only one or two fell at first and then more and more. They landed in the ditch and on the shoulder. One crashed onto the truck's bed and bounced off the back. The truck screeched and fishtailed and wobbled at high speed down the highway.

Another cow, probably the largest, fell directly in front of the pickup.

SPEED
LIMIT
55

a siren bawled outside just before dawn, and he rushed past meredith, who was smashing new cranberry pieces she'd stolen that morning

the cranberry shards on the floor repeatedly cut his bare feet, but he felt no pain, just pressure as if he were only stepping on round pebbles

he looked down – in each piece of glass was a tiny meredith face crying at him

he kept walking, heard the skin of his feet puncturing and slicing open

he stood in the sticky warmth of his blood that pulse-puddled out from him

the breakfast nook rattled and danced, the house shook and moaned in the dark winds that smashed the windows and ripped the curtains from the rods, and trees lining the lake fell all around and made snapping and banging sounds that were louder than the chugging roar that closed in on everything

the roar might have been the rain pouring in the broken windows, might have been the sugarberry that fell on the shed in what seemed to be lingering slow motion, or maybe the lake whirlpooling in waves bigger than the aluminum fishing boats that usually reflected the summer sun

or it might have been the lightning – this lightning was like no other lightning he'd ever seen...it wasn't purplish-blue – it was pink, and a little bit red, and a mix of green like gumballs, and orange

SPEED
LIMIT
55

MAYFIELD JAMMED BOTH feet down hard on the spongy brake pedal and threw the wheel to the right. The truck skidded around the cow, but the front fender glanced the rump and twisted away.

The truck, still careening, shot off the shoulder and tore up the grass of a historical wayside. It was the only green grass Mayfield had seen in several scorching months. The wayside's marker sign splintered and crumbled away underneath the front bumper.

The truck smashed into a long, flat boulder that had a copper plaque imbedded in it. The front and back wheels tore away with a sickening crunch. The pickup's body sailed with the wind up and over the rock as pieces of the wheels, suspension system, and floor of the cab bounced across the ground.

Paperbacks ripped apart and spread their yellowed pages over the chained picnic tables. The pages were Yokley smiles all across the sky.

What was left of the truck plummeted and spun along in the mud as the tornado dissolved back into the storm.

Mayfield sat there for a minute in the cab and thought about how his feet could have been crushed into the ground like cigarettes in an ashtray if he hadn't stomped both on the brake pedal and kept them there. His mind was in high gear, but he didn't know what else he was supposed to think or feel or even whether or not his heart was supposed to be racing on account of his narrow escape.

His feet itched, so he kicked off his shoes and rubbed his soles on what was left of the remaining footwell's dirty truck carpet until they were warm and tingling.

SPEED
LIMIT
55

the morning air was damp and cool, the sky was windburn-bright, and a swath of woods around the little lake had been brushed aside to make room for nothing

he and meredith stood together and looked at the mangled shed under the fallen sugarberry, asking each other with no words how they survived

a moment of clarity for her, rare recently — meredith shook her head, and the only time in all the years they were married mayfield heard her pray —

'though I walk through the valley beside still waters'

SPEED
LIMIT
55

EXCEPT FOR STEAM wheezing out the radiator and rain splashing in the cab, everything was silent. A ripped page fluttered on the dashboard. It was white and regal, one corner lifting and falling as the breeze that was left from the wind toyed with it. Mayfield picked it up and examined it.

A slash of shark-teeth horror. It was not a page from a paperback. The paper was too crisp and smooth, not rough and yellowing, and was blank except for a box for an endorsement. Mayfield turned the paper over, and his own handwriting on the other side stoked the flint-spark horror in him to a roaring flame.

$11,653.

The check he made out to the funeral home.

Mayfield stared at the numbers, lost track of time, blinked only when his eyes flared dry, swallowed tentatively in a series of gulps that grew in resolve until the flaming horror was stamped down.

He folded the check and put it in his shirt pocket.

An absinthe bottle was teetering on the front edge of the crumpled hood. Mayfield shifted in the driver's seat, and the bottle fell. Mayfield knew it smashed because the sound was loud and clear through the shattered windshield.

The box they'd stolen from the diner back in North Carolina, three bottles remaining in it, was still in the truck bed. So were the crutches they'd stolen from Andalusia. The truck bed was like a shark cage. Or a tornado cage. Or like a race car roll cage. Only Yokley's books and one bottle had slipped through, and the crutches and the box with the other bottles had been protected even from the falling cow.

Mayfield remained in the cab for just another minute or so. He looked out at the flat countryside. The land around him seemed reallocated, like an unsmoothed tablecloth.

No sign of Yokley.

He always said he'd go far, Mayfield thought.

A grove of blown-down trees to the left, another cow carcass to the right, and straight ahead, off in the distance, a white farmhouse completely intact surrounded by rubble of barns, machinery, and sheds.

He got out to look for a payphone at the wayside. He hoped there still was a phone there. If not blown away, then still there in a past time because this trip felt to Mayfield as if it had been happening in a previous decade. Why wouldn't there be a payphone?

A Cadillac with tinted windows slowed on the highway and tooted its horn, but Mayfield waved it on, and it sped off and was soon over the horizon.

No payphone.

Mayfield sat under the picnic shelter at an old wooden table. He picked at its flaking green paint, toed some dirt, and made his plan for going home.

Why did he wave the Cadillac on? He now beat himself up over that because he had no idea what to do. He had no idea where he was. He might as well start walking. No doubt fixing the truck was out of the question.

A bank. That's what he needed. A bank to make a withdrawal. An airport. A plane ticket.

The direction the Cadillac had gone. That's where he'd go. That was the best course. Someone else had to come along sooner or later. Hitch a ride. Yes.

He stood and raised his head toward the truck for a last look. It had brought him from a point in Georgia to this point here in Nebraska, more than a thousand miles between. It deserved a last look.

A cloud of lips floated like gnats above the truck's smashed-in front grill.

Mayfield said to himself, "Mad men know nothing…"

—so the tornado hadn't pulled the lips up and away to the other side of a mirror, or over the fucking rainbow—

"…why will you say that I am mad?"

Yokley had quoted that at him the other day.

Mayfield sagged in defeat like a man who has just been told his car has been repossessed or that he's been summoned to court.

Or that his wife can no longer live at home.

Nothing about this trip had been rejuvenating. He hadn't slept well in any of the motels — the mattresses were springy and saggy. Mayfield's back ached worse. One tooth throbbed the same as always. He was tired and not sure where he wanted to be today. He felt as old and vacant as he deserved to feel, but he knew everyone would say it was a miracle he wasn't hurt.

The center of the lip cloud darkened to a deeper shade of red, like a number in a color blindness test, and Mayfield saw a pair of glinting, shiny shoes in that more blood-like shade.

The whole lip cloud swirled to the shape of a hand. An index finger. The finger beckoned come here.

The lips separated into four fingers. Each finger darted to a wheel well, spun into wheel shapes, and hoisted the truck. Ready to roll.

SPEED
LIMIT
55

FOURTEEN HOURS LATER, in the black hours before dawn, Mayfield was pulled over just outside Tenaha, Texas. He ached everywhere from so much driving in such a hurry. He shook because he was hungry and thirsty and because he was on the powerful verge of forgetting all this.

The deputy was a paunchy, middle-aged man with a pockmarked face and a permanent smirk that aggrandized his Louisiana accent.

Yes, he was born and raised in Natchitoches, Mayfield intuited, and somehow ended up doomed to this life one state away.

The deputy shone his flashlight in the banged-up truck bed and asked Mayfield about the crutches.

Mayfield told him he used them months ago for an ankle injury that was still slowing him down, and he hadn't taken them out of the truck since.

The deputy asked Mayfield to step out after remarking that the crutches looked kind of old fashioned, and Mayfield did so wincing and favoring an ankle while explaining he had borrowed them from his mother, who used them years ago and never got rid of them.

The officer asked him where he was from and where he was going.

Mayfield said, "Slippery Rock," and "California, maybe,

after some family time in Tombstone."

Mayfield opened the box without being asked to.

Under the deputy's flashlight, the green absinthe in the three remaining bottles glowed like treasure behind a waterfall.

The deputy straightened in excitement there in the dark on the side of the road, Louisiana swamp calls deep and guttural ahead of them just across the state line where Mayfield had never been and lucky Texas cattle lowing sweet and sad far, far behind past the horizon, and he reached for a bottle.

Mayfield let him have it.

In less than a minute, Mayfield was politely saying good-bye and thank you and was accelerating down the highway again on his way to the Georgia coast. The center lines were reliable and reassuring, and no one else was on the road. The lip tires were humming softly. The bluish-gray ink of dawn was spreading out against the sky. There was lots of time for making plans now that he'd accounted for every last marble after spilling them, even the ones rolled under hard-to-reach places, and he was making plans to park the truck near a beach house, leave the crutches, scuttle across the sand into the sea, and release himself to the waves.

THE TENNESSEE SCRAMBLER

TEMPTED AND TRIED IS HOW I'd describe it. It was so funny. On Tuesday afternoon, I found the first note nailed to the front door of my little house on Mud Lick Ridge. It was the first really hot day of summer, ninety-six degrees, oppressively humid down in the valley but cooler up on the mountain, and it hadn't rained anywhere in east Tennessee since the beginning of April. Or so I heard from the townspeople.

The note had been written on a piece of a cereal box with a picture of a green elf on it. It read *Stay away from Violet* in chicken-scratch red pencil handwriting that crisscrossed the elf's face like razor cuts.

I threw the note in the kitchen trash and forgot about it. Normally I wouldn't have been nonchalant about a cryptic warning nailed to my door, but, to tell you the truth, it really didn't alarm me much. I didn't know anyone named Violet. I was new in town and figured nobody knew me well enough either to have a bone to pick with me already. Perhaps whoever left the note thought the previous occupant of my house was still living there.

So I didn't think about the note again until I came home from Francesca's the next night and found *another* one nailed to the door in the same spot. This one had been written on a folded sheet of legal paper in the same red pencil handwriting. *What does it take to get you to listen?*

Puzzling. I sat down and rubbed my knee. The cool spot Francesca had put in it when she first touched me there a few weeks ago flipped and fluttered under my skin like a trout skimming just below the surface of a stream. It grew cold sometimes at odd moments like this. But it wasn't unwelcome.

I poured myself a Hendricks & tonic, sliced a lime, and went out front. The fireflies bobbed above the swaying brown grass. The moon was rising through the white oaks. My rocking chair creaked on the wooden porch. The mountain grew dark and full of night sounds. Cicadas and raccoons. Owls and witch ghosts. I checked the deadbolt on the door and went to bed soon after I finished my drink, my knee feeling tight and cold all night long.

A third note showed up on Thursday, when a fire advisory was posted for all of Orion County and the surrounding area. Written on the torn-off back cover of a paperback romance novel, this one read *Didn't I tell you to stay away from her?*

HIGH NOON FRIDAY afternoon in Lawton, Tennessee, is always quiet in the summer. The flashing sign at the bank said ninety-eight. All three of the notes were in my back pocket. I walked down the empty street past the post office and the flag hanging limp on the pole. You often hear something spooky must be going on in a sleepy Southern town near the mountains, that there are thrilling secrets lurking everywhere about to spill out from behind all the church steeples, painted white storefronts, and crumbling depots. But if you could call this mysterious — an old man chewing tobacco and playing checkers by himself while sitting on an upside-down washtub out front of Godfrey's Market — then I guess Lawton is the kind of place you'd want to gossip about.

Anyhow, it was just a hop, skip, and a jump to the sheriff's office and the green water tower on the edge of town. A few miles past that, Mud Lick Ridge towered over the valley, blurry in the haze. It was a strangely shaped mountain, rolling and round on the south end but with an enormous shale and sandstone outcropping on the north end that looked like a prow with a figurehead hanging over steep rocky cliffs.

An older woman I knew only as Miriam came out of the flower shop and stopped me. She was carrying a bouquet of orange pompon dahlias in a green vase. You might describe her as pleasantly plump, and she wouldn't mind.

"Grand prize in the quilting club raffle is a beauty, Clinton," she said. "Chocolate chip cookie the size of a Volkswagen. Made by Thelma Ogelthorpe." She shook some water off her fingers. "Best try buying ten tickets if you want a chance of winning it. Funny, ain't it? I'd never drive a Volkswagen. Foreign piece of you-know-what. But a cookie the *size* of a Volkswagen? Made by Thelma?" Miriam closed her eyes and went *mmm mmm*. She touched my arm and said, "How's your mama doing?" Her fingers were still a little wet from the water on the flowers.

My knee tightened and went colder. It felt like a plucked banjo string trembling with a fading note that warbled up and down my leg and went quiet until plucked again. Every now and then, whatever it was, that cold spot from Francesca's fingers made its own slow, tingly music in its own time.

"Fine, considering," I said. "Dad…Daddy, didn't really leave her much of anything except the house, and she won't sell that either. But she misses him too much to dwell on what she might do with it."

"Aw," Miriam said. "I still remember when your mama and me was just itty bitty girls. How she used to just love the mountain fairies. She chased after them at night, tried to catch them with her precious little net and little old jar. But they was too fast for her. Say, you look just like your mama too. Reckon folks here asking if you're kin to her."

"All the time," I said. "Just about every day." I thanked Miriam and continued on my way.

"Don't forget the raffle," I heard her call from behind me. I turned and waved.

Now Mama is never one to admit she needs anything. She's stubborn. She wasn't going to leave Evanston and her Tudor-style house overlooking Lake Michigan, no, she wasn't going to move anywhere else just because Dad had died. She was going to stay close to his grave, she said.

I've always believed that signs nudge us and whisper to

us how someone we don't see or talk to that often is doing, what they're thinking, what they're up to. The cool spot on my knee, the one Francesca had left, had grown colder just then on the hot sidewalk talking with Miriam. And Miriam had asked about Mama. Maybe that was my sign I should call her again soon, though I'd only been in Lawton a little while, not more than a few weeks.

My knee loosened up a bit and the coolness faded as I walked some more.

The grass was lying dead between the sidewalk and the street in dry, dusty clumps, and kudzu hung from a grove of hickory trees next to the drug store & soda fountain where I picked up some beans, rice, and cornbread every afternoon at lunchtime. I went in. A bell jangled from a string tied to the door handle.

Only two people were in the dim, cool place today. One, Della Frasier, sat at the end of the counter next to the window, opposite the grill. She looked up and eyed me with suspicion. Her overalls were tucked into her gray wool socks that came up as high as her knees. Her Birkenstocks were falling apart. Her brown hair, streaked with silver, was braided into pigtails that came down to her waist. A bar of blue shadow from a telephone pole outside crossed her face. I'd seen her before. She seemed to be in the drug store & soda fountain every time I stopped in. Just about everyone in town was saying this Della Frasier was crazy. She continued eating her cereal, swished the milk around in the bowl, and watched me sideways.

The second woman, Dot, was about the same age as Della but prettier with straight silver hair pulled back into a ponytail, smooth napkin-white skin, and eyes so blue they jumped from her face.

"Morning, new guy in town," Dot said, smiling.

One thing you'll notice about Dot is her apron is always clean, even after she's spent an hour grilling hamburgers and bacon popping in grease. The first time I went in there, the day after I'd finished settling into my new office, Dot had looked up from her pot of collard greens, and the first thing out of her mouth was if I was kin to my mama. She volunteered to show me around Lawton right then and there. She said toodle doo to the last lingering old men from the lunch crowd, took her apron off and threw it over the cash register, and walked out of the place with her arm hooked in mine. She led me back behind the tiny business district, where stately bed & breakfasts with columns in front lined the road and a stream bubbled down through a park with a gazebo. The streets were still, but faces—moons of cotton—peeked through blank windows as we passed houses and storefronts on our way back through downtown.

Della Frasier dropped her spoon in her bowl. A little milk splashed onto the counter. The cereal box next to the bowl went into her empty denim sack. She got up, swung the sack over her shoulder, threw a neatly folded bill and a handful of coins down, and strode out, giving me a surly look right in the eye. The door swung shut with the little bell tinkling.

"Don't mind her none," Dot said. "She's just a little crazy, is all."

"Brings her own cereal every day, does she?" I said.

Dot nodded and made a *yep* expression with her eyebrows. "Don't like our kind, I guess. What can I get you?"

"Any red velvet cake left from yesterday?"

Dot grabbed my shoulders and smiled. "Is my name not Violet Dorothy Owen? Damned if I ain't been saving a piece for you."

SPEED
LIMIT
55

YOU MIGHT CALL me a wayfaring stranger. Mama always said she named me Clinton Harrell Bloomington after a boy from Mississippi she heard about. Apparently this boy moved north just so he could swim all the way across Lake Michigan. And he did too. By himself. Several times, if Mama's not exaggerating. Funny thing about Mama, she does. And she always starts her stories with *It was so funny*. That's your cue that she's got something to say and that you're going to listen for a while. I'm not sure why that story about the Mississippi boy always stuck with Mama, but the significance of the name weighed me down all my life. It gave me an inkling, maybe just like that boy who left Mississippi, that I'd be *going*. That that's what I was meant to do, only I'd be going in a different direction than the one the first Clinton Harrell took. Even when I was young, I felt guilty about knowing that Chicago just didn't feel like the right place for me, knowing someday I'd leave the old hot dog wagon on the corner, the parks along the lake, the tree-lined avenues, and the big houses and nice lawns of Evanston. The comfort. If there is such a thing.

After lunch, I dropped the notes off at the sheriff's office. He wasn't in. His deputy, on the other hand, looked like he had nothing better to do but, well, wait around for something better to do. He was tired and bored, his feet up on the desk while he picked at his teeth with a toothpick and talked on the phone. His bald spot was burned a bright red.

I waited for the deputy to finish his conversation.

"Went to see Duke Watson this morning and ask him if I could borrow his old bloodhound Mary Beth," the deputy said into the phone. "But Mary Beth got tangled up with a rattler under the porch yesterday afternoon. She sure fought, says Duke Watson, but that rattler bit her in forty places. Now Duke Watson's known for stretching a tale a bit far, but it sure was a damn sorrowful sight to see that old man crying over his dead dog like that."

Finally, the deputy hung up and asked me what I wanted.

"The sheriff," he said, "is over at the fairgrounds, watching them set things up, making sure everything's up to code and all." The deputy's name tag under his badge read Leonard Sneed. He took the three notes from me and filed them away with a short report, saying only "We'll look into this, I reckon," and he started picking his teeth again as if these kinds of notes popped up all the time in Lawton. Like paper funeral home fans or something.

Anyway, my two afternoon appointments ended early, so Francesca came and met me at the office. I left my car there, and we got in her huge lemon-yellow convertible and headed up Mud Lick Ridge with the top down. What a gorgeous car she had. Clean. Shiny. Sleek chrome bumpers. The brown vinyl seats were in fine condition still, and the spokes glittered as if they'd just been polished. And the gleaming paint on that old Buick wasn't faded from the Tennessee sun like most of the other cars I'd seen around town.

The warm wind whistled around us as we sped up the mountain. Francesca liked to drive fast. Whenever her mama or stepdad told her to drive careful—their way of saying goodbye—she always replied *No, I want to drive reckless.* We sailed around a blind curve, tires squealing.

I've always said (and Mama agreed) that the right woman for me would be the one who didn't flinch or shriek when I drove through hills like those in Tennessee. But it's another story when you're the one riding and someone else is driving. Going around the next hairpin turn, we almost hit head on a rusty old pickup truck that had crossed the center line and was coming straight for us. But Francesca swerved around it just in time, and I of course grabbed for the armrest. The other driver's only reaction was a small wave, just a quick lift of his finger off the steering wheel really.

Francesca slowed for the next curve, swung out of it, and the speedometer jumped into the seventies again. The trees and bushes lining the road blurred by, and an outcropping of crumbling shale. Francesca braked once more and eased us around another curve going left. To our right was the guardrail, as well as a breathtaking view of Lawton and the valley far below.

We passed the crushed rock driveway leading up into the woods to my house. Soon we reached the top of the mountain, where Francesca turned off onto a side road. Pebbles crunched under the tires. It was cooler and darker on this road through the black oaks, and bugs swarmed in clouds. By then, I'd loosened my hold on the armrest. She tucked some of her curly red hair behind her ear.

A three-legged deer bounced across in front of us. Its tail flittered away through the trees.

"Must have got hit," Francesca said.

We came to the abandoned logging camp, climbed out of the car, and sat together on the back bumper. The motor ticked. She put her hand on my knee, and the cool spot she'd planted there when we first met a few weeks ago grew slowly, shrank a bit, and grew again. It was a pleasant moment of enjoying her lilac perfume, listening to the squirrels, feeling the added warmth of the sun when it occasionally poked its way through the breezy shade.

I have to tell you, in case I haven't already, that Orion County is a dry county. Francesca had to go over the dam to Ainsworth County just for a bottle of white zinfandel. We poured it in plastic cups and ate the strawberry pineapple tarts I'd bought from the bakery after the sheriff's office.

Francesca was in a talkative mood.

"I want to tell you about a road trip I took a long time ago," she said, "when I was seventeen. I ran off with my boyfriend Roddie. He was twenty. We left in his old Mustang in the middle of the night. That was so silly. His car was loud. It woke everybody up in the neighborhood, including Mama and my stepdaddy. They rushed out on the porch in their pajamas, yelling for me to come back before they rented out my room to somebody who was grateful for it. Roddie and I just sped away. It was a humid night, late in July, I think. I imagine we must have left a cloud of blue smoke lingering behind. We were gone a week. We made it as far as Alamogordo, no destination in mind. We just wanted to go where we went, and Alamogordo was where the car broke down and we had a big fight, and where Roddie brushed his long hair out of his eyes, smoked his Kools one after another, and told me I had too much baggage. I walked to a grocery store down the street from the motel, called my stepdaddy in tears trying not to let on I was crying, the full moon shining down on me from the big, clear New Mexico sky, and I was too scared to ask him to wire me money for a ticket home."

I listened without saying anything. Occasionally I nodded or touched her hair. The cool spot on my knee felt like a patch of frozen lake covered with fresh snow. The spot was growing colder little by little now until she finally pulled her hand away and it started to warm just a bit.

Some days, I didn't notice this cool spot at all. Other times, it would pulse in time to music. But mostly it was there but not really. At first, I thought maybe it was some kind of nerve problem I'd never studied before and that it would flare up only every once in a while. But soon I realized my knee usually felt coolest when Francesca put her hand on it, and this coolness would sometimes spread until it went up and down my leg too. Plus, there were a few other occasions when it would do that when she wasn't around, like when Miriam asked how Mama was doing. Whatever it was, I didn't worry about it too much because it was kind of pleasing. In a way.

The late afternoon crept on by, and Francesca and I stayed quiet on the bumper a long time. We poured more wine. The sounds of the woods surrounded us.

She started talking again.

"So I spent my summers by Charleston at my daddy's

beach house on Isle of Palms. I used to feed the gulls that came and sat on the deck railing. Other kids were always running around in the sand and playing. I remember one year there was a hurricane coming the last week of August, right before school started. Lines of idling cars stretched forever in front of Daddy's Lincoln. Both lanes of the highway clogged with traffic moving in the same direction, away from the coming storm. Nobody was going into Charleston. And the fumes, oh. I remember the wipers slashing away the few raindrops that were beginning to come down from the sky. And I sat in the front seat, my book closed in my lap, and I watched Daddy. He always sat so still, his eyes locked on the trunk of the car in front of us. His arms were big, almost as big around as scuba tanks, that's how big they were. His anchor tattoo showed through the sleeve of his T-shirt. I loved that tattoo. And you know what? That's the last day I ever spent with my daddy."

We finished the wine and lingered there a while longer after she was done with her story. I tried to imagine what the old logging camp must have been like back when it was still being used, who must have worked there, whatever happened to everyone. And you always have the feeling that something is watching you too when you're in the woods. But there was nothing except the abandoned camp, birds chittering, leaves rustling, brief silence when everything quieted down for a moment. After we got back in the car, Francesca's description of her father's tattoo stayed with me while we drove in the dusk toward my house a little ways down the mountain.

In the corner of my eye, a flash of purple followed by a

flash of pink. The fireflies were coming out, fireflies of all colors. But they didn't sparkle and fade, like usual. They stayed bright in dazzling brilliance, in bursts of pink, purple, green, and blue. They spun, darted, wove in and between the bushes, trees, and undergrowth, looped up and down, left trails of fading light behind them.

I'm only going over Jordan, Francesca sang softly to herself, as she liked to do, while we were pulling up my driveway. The scent of mountain laurel and her lilac perfume was strong around us, whippoorwills were calling, and the cool spot on my knee where she liked to touch me still shimmered like a phantom. *I'm only going over home…*

We walked up my porch steps together. A ripped-off paperback cover was nailed to my front door again. Only this time nothing was written on it.

SPEED
LIMIT
55

FRANCESCA AND I made plans to stay at Star Falls Creek and Lake Chickamahonny the next day, Saturday. Her mama and stepdad had an old place up there on the water that we could use for the rest of the weekend.

Lake Chickamahonny has an interesting history. Years and years ago, some rich businessman from Atlanta had the idea that it would be nice to make a lake in the middle of the woods near his summer house, so he quickly bought up all the land he could at outrageous prices, bulldozed a bunch of trees and cottages, hollowed out a huge depression where Star Falls Creek ran through with water from the river, let it fill, and stocked it with rockfish, largemouth bass, and catfish. The lake is now about four and a half acres in size, twenty feet deep in its deepest spot.

Not long after, when they had to move the railroad track on account of the quarry, they built a trestle for the new track over the west end of the lake. Francesca was always telling me she slept best at her mama and stepdad's old place because the trains went by in the night.

Anywhere else it was just too quiet for sleep, she said.

Apparently the Atlanta businessman also left a few old cottages where they were in the lower areas to be flooded instead of bulldozing them. Somewhere on the bottom of the lake, they remain exactly as they were abandoned, filled, I suppose, with furniture and other possessions that might have been left behind. I don't think anybody ever tried looking for them, but after Francesca told me this story I often pictured those cottages down there in the murky water among gnarled stumps, flooded up past ceilings and roofs, sofas and iceboxes and beds and cabinets and dining room tables set with chipped dishes and silverware all visited only by the fish now.

When I was a kid, I wanted to be a fisherman. Something about the water always drew me to it. I took a year off between high school and college to work on a crab boat in Alaska. The smell of fresh fish, bilge water, wet salt, and diesel fumes made me retch and hang over the railing constantly those first few days, sore in the chest from endless gagging and dry heaving. I couldn't get used to the smell, and the tough, scraggly skipper always had something to holler about.

Until one day when he was down on deck watching us

empty the nets. I'd cut my arm deep on some sharp, rusty wire sticking out from a lantern down below, and it was bleeding and raw in the chilly ocean spray. I wasn't working as fast as I should have been, and when the skipper got on my case about it I simply dropped what I was doing without saying anything back to him, and I went down to the galley. He followed me, screaming the whole way for me to get back up top. When I got to the galley door, I turned around, grabbed him by the throat while he was in mid yell, and shoved him against the wall so hard the lantern went out and he sputtered. I was a good head taller than him. His tongue stuck out where he had no teeth. He stank of fish, sweat, and oil. He tried prying my fingers loose from his leathery neck, but I held on to him tight and told him I'd throw him overboard if he said anything more about it.

Just as quickly as I grabbed him I let him go, and he stumbled away down the pitching passageway, looking behind at me, rubbing his neck. I expected him to fire me. But he never said a word about it, and he never bothered me again. I kept working the nets, sometimes asking myself over and over why I'd really snapped at him like that, sometimes thinking of home instead, and the lake and Mama's summer tea with lemons and her constant corrections and words of wisdom and old wives' tales, and of Dad coming home in the evenings from his histology lab with his white coat reeking of formaldehyde, of his perpetual silence and whatever he must have been hiding in that marriage-and-mortgage-weary head of his. I couldn't help being curious.

And it started getting cold early that year when I was on the crab boat. Too cold. But I stuck with it a couple months despite the constant ache in my back, neck, and shoulders, the frozen feeling in my fingers and joints that never seemed to go away, and the endless hours chipping ice off the boat so it wouldn't get top heavy and overturn. I never went back out on a fishing boat like that again, but every now and then I still fancied myself a sailor, if only for the romance of the whole thing.

It smelled smoky outside when Francesca and I drove back down to the valley in the morning mountain fog early Saturday to pick up my car in town. Where there's smoke there's fire, they say. Only down here people say it so it sounds like far. Where there's smoke there's far. And Francesca drove more carefully than yesterday. The fog grew thinner as we made our way farther down the winding mountain highway.

"The ground's been so dry lately," Francesca said, "the trees have been bribing the dogs."

"Hotter than a goat's butt in a pepper patch," I said, remembering one of Mama's favorite sayings.

The fog dissipated shortly before the bottom of the mountain. We rolled into town and pulled in the parking lot at my office, where I tried to start my car. But the engine wouldn't turn over. No lights on the dashboard even. I got out and checked under the hood, and, lo and behold, the battery was missing.

"What could have happened to it?" Francesca said. We stood there a minute, staring at the empty spot where the battery had been, at the cables that hung loose now, and we looked at each other and shrugged.

"Looks like somebody took it," I said.

"Well, we have my car," she said.

I glanced around. It was still early, still cool. No traffic came down the street. The town was empty. The only other car in the parking lot was an ancient and dirty Ford Fairmont over by the dumpster. The car was missing its hubcaps. Curious, I walked over and peeked in. A clipboard and a yellow legal pad rested on the dashboard. The pages were faded and curled. A crumpled, grease-stained bag from the drive-in was jammed in the ashtray. Old yellow paperbacks, some with covers missing, littered the floor in front of the passenger seat.

"Look," Francesca called from behind me. "There's blood."

Della Frasier jumped up from behind the Fairmont so fast you might have thought she'd been bitten on the heel by a possum.

"You the doctor?" she said. Her voice was high and tinny, almost like a squeak. I'd expected it to be low and sandy. She held a blood-soaked towel to her head, stood hunched over, obviously in pain, one hand holding the towel, one hand in her pocket. She wore the same overalls and wool socks she'd been wearing at the drug store & soda fountain the day before. She seemed fidgety and nervous, like she'd been caught doing something she wasn't supposed to.

"Come on in," I told her, "and I'll have a look at you."

I motioned to Francesca, led Della Frasier to the rear door next to the dumpster, took out my keys, and unlocked my office. The two of us went down the long dark hallway past the bathroom and refrigerator in the back to my exam room in front. I flipped on the lights. Della Frasier got up on the table, moaning.

"What happened to you," I said.

"I hit my head."

She was even more nervous now, eyes shifting around my exam room, arms shaking, feet swinging back and forth. I took her hand away from the towel, which was completely soaked through bright red. I removed the towel from her head and bent her down closer to me so I could see. She had a long straight cut in her scalp, deep and still oozing fresh blood through her hair and the blood that had already clotted. The cut ran three inches halfway down the side of her head and ended just above her ear, and the surrounding skin was already swollen.

"What did you hit your head on?" I said. "Or did someone hit you?"

"I can't afford to pay you nothing."

"We'll work that out later."

"Except maybe I could give you some chickens or a pail of blueberries."

"We need to get this taken care of."

"You like blueberries?" she said, tilting her head back up again so she could look at me.

A couple of long dark hairs were sprouting from her chin. Her eyes were gray and hard. And she smelled like macaroni & cheese. But she relaxed a little when I told her my mama used to give me bowls of frozen blueberries bought fresh from the farmers market. She'd freeze them and mix them with cream in summertime when the afternoons passed so slowly the lake waves stood still. I'd take my bowl down to the beach just a hundred yards or so from our house, and I'd sit on the sand and eat spoonful after spoonful of those glorious icy berries while the lake gelled under the hot summer sun. A little bit of home, Mama always said.

And I started thinking more about Mama just then while I was telling Della Frasier about the frozen blueberries and cream, and I realized I'd forgotten to call her the night before like I told myself I would. But maybe it was good that I hadn't called. Mama no doubt would have started talking about how nice the boy who mowed the lawn was, how sweet the old man who brought her her groceries was (maybe he was trying to get fresh with her, she'd also say), and she'd segue into how nice it would be to have her own son home to do those things for her, just like Mrs. Proudfit's son came over in his new Mercedes every night after work to check on his mother and see if she needed anything. At that point, Mama would sigh and ask no one in particular, though she was speaking to me, what she did to deserve living alone now. But I tried to cut her some slack—it had been only a few weeks, after all—and Mama only needed some time to settle into a new routine.

I remember when Mama first told me I was going to be a doctor. One year, when I was about twelve, Mama took Dad and me to help our neighbor sell his tomatoes and green peppers from his garden at the Evanston farmers market on the Fourth of July. It was so hot that day. The new blacktop on the street bubbled, and people walked around sipping lemonade they'd bought by the goat cheese and pesto stand. Dad stood around all morning with his hands in his pockets. Mama was wearing her peacock-feather hat. She cooed and clucked with her friends whenever they ambled by. Our neighbor only sat in a canvas chair with his legs crossed. He scratched his neck and rubbed his whiskers. I made change and handed people their bags.

A little girl with curly blond hair, blue eyes, and sunburned skin toddled past our vegetables, bumped into a Doberman on a leash tied to a maple nearby, and dropped her paper cone of lemonade. She squealed and held her sticky hands out to pet the dog.

The dog, slick as an alewife slipping away after being thrown back in the water, flashed its teeth, chomped her ear, and tore it off. In one swallow, the ear was gone, and blood dyed the little girl's blue jumper brown.

She still reached for the dog, unaware of what it had done. Blood oozed down her face like sticky paint and soaked into her jumper like spilled chocolate milk on a tablecloth. The Doberman gazed at her, showed its teeth again, and snarled.

I watched, stunned in surprise at first. I didn't move. Mama's friend Cora Abelman from the herb club, who was buying cider at the next booth, screamed longer and sharper than anyone I ever heard scream before. Her scream kicked my feet in motion and propelled me to the girl. I tripped over a jug of cider Cora Abelman had dropped in her shock, but I lost no time. When I reached the girl and picked her up, she was bawling, yelling, jumping up and down, holding her hand to her ear.

Someone shouted, and the dog barked, leaped, strained against its leash, snapping at the girl and me. I turned so the girl couldn't see the dog, stepped around the maple, set her down on some grass behind a bush.

"Let me look," I remember telling her, trying my best to

smile in a reassuring way.

The dog continued barking, the girl kept shrieking, and a crowd of people gathered around us.

"Give me your handkerchief," I said to Cora Abelman. She handed it to me with shaky fingers, and she stood there crying and wiping away tears with her other hand. I took her handkerchief, pressed it to the girl's ear. She was kicking now and still hollering.

"Yes, that was a mean dog, wasn't it?" I said to her.

A tall, thin man ran up from somewhere, identified himself as a doctor, kneeled next to the girl and took a look at the blood on her face, her shoulder, and her jumper. He told someone to call for an ambulance, and he scooped the girl up and ran her across the street to the pharmacy.

Mama insisted on taking a picture of me while I stood there awkwardly and the crowd thinned. In all the excitement, nobody thought to check on the dog or make sure it didn't get away. I broke from Mama, my dad, and our neighbor, and I went back to see if there was a name tag on the collar. But the dog was gone. Its leash was still tied to the maple, its collar still attached. No tag.

"You look like your mama," Della Frasier said.

"So I've heard," I said. I soaped up and washed my hands. "We're going to clean you up here," I continued, "and get you stitched up."

"Stitches?" she said, eyes wide, hairs sticking straight out of her chin.

"Probably about fifteen of them," I said. "You really hurt yourself."

Francesca came into the exam room just as I poured a few

drops of sterile water on Della Frasier's wound. Della Frasier flinched and stiffened. She twisted the end of one of her long pigtails around her wrist.

"I need to talk with you," Francesca said, staring at me tightly and ignoring Della Frasier. Generally she wouldn't have interrupted me while I was with a patient, so I gave Della Frasier a clean towel and went out to the hallway to see what she wanted.

"You should see this," was all she said, and she led me back outside to my car. The hood was still propped open. Francesca pointed, and just under the corner and a few inches along the underside of the hood was a smear of fresh blood. Francesca pointed at the bumper and headlight, which were splashed with a few small drops of blood too. Even the blacktop was splattered, but the blood blended with it so well it was no wonder we hadn't seen it before. I followed the trail of blood drops across the parking lot with my eyes. They led back toward the dusty Ford Fairmont by the dumpster. I walked over there, put two and two together, clenched my fists, gritted my teeth, and…shook my head and looked up at the sky.

Like Mama always did when us kids got in trouble.

And I thought, Just what did that damn Della Frasier think she was doing?

don't mind her none

What the hell did she want to go steal my car battery for

she's just a little crazy, is all

And I got so mad right then…

I saw her back at the lunch counter at the drug store & soda grill, sitting there splashing the milk in her cereal bowl, putting that neatly folded bill and a handful of change down, taking her cereal box in her denim sack, running her tongue over her teeth while she swaggered out giving me the evil eye.

you the doctor you like blueberries can't afford to pay you nothing

damned if i ain't been saving a piece for you is my name not violet dorothy owen

I looked in the Ford Fairmont again. There they were, the paperback novels, some with covers missing.

And it all made sense now.

don't like our kind i guess

stitches i could give you some chickens

The hood had come down on her head. That's what happened, all right.

…yeah, I got so mad right then I wanted to kill her.

But I thought of something better.

MAMA USED TO take things from my sister and me. That was how she punished us. When Willadeene and I were cleaning out one of Dad's closets the day after his funeral, we found a box full of our old things. Like Willadeene's cowgirl doll from Wall Drug, my battered Superman pop-up book, our Looney Tunes record, an Alcatraz snow globe that Dad had brought home for Willadeene from a convention trip to California, my spinning geisha music box from New York that tinkled "A More Humane Mikado," and many, many more things, like my slingshot, Willadeene's first

Valentine's Day card from a boy, my little fifth-grade picture book that had no signatures in it because Mama made me stay home the last week of school when she was in bed with one of her many illnesses, my glass dolphin from a glassworks shop in Atlantic City, and on and on, all things Willadeene and I had had some attachment to a long time ago.

Together we brought the box to Mama and set it down before her on the breakfast nook table. She was still in her nightgown and slippers, and her hair was wrapped in a green silk scarf. We told her we wanted to know what the box had been doing in Dad's closet, but Mama just stirred her tea without answering and looked tearfully out the window at Lake Michigan rolling its waves toward us like dice.

AT FIRST, IT wasn't hard convincing Della Frasier she didn't need any anesthetic for the stitches. Not for a minor cut like that. Only those with life-threatening injuries needed anesthetic, Francesca and I reassured her while we washed our hands. And this was no life-threatening injury. Not by a long shot.

And besides, we both said, it wouldn't hurt at all. Not a bit.

She relaxed, apparently relieved that it wasn't as serious as she'd worried. How lucky she was, she said. But she still wouldn't admit how she'd hurt herself. So we laid her down on her back on the examining room table, and I got started, moving quickly. The first suture only went partway in before Della Frasier recoiled with a loud Ow. Her hand snapped to her head, and she glared at me.

At the same time, the cold spot in my knee tingled and intensified. "Ow ow ow," Della Frasier said again.

I flexed my leg and shifted my weight to my other one. "Now you have to lie still," I said. "We can't have no more of this here crying, or it's bound to get infected."

"Infected?" she said.

"That's right, infected," Francesca said. "And you'll have to take all kinds of medicines until it gets better."

"Medicines?"

I pulled her hand away from her head and pricked her again.

"Ow!"

"What did I just tell you?" I said.

My knee felt like it had a frozen acrobat squeeze puppet inside doing back flips and somersaults.

"But it hurts," Della Frasier said.

I tried one more time to get that suture in, but Della Frasier rolled away from me and hopped off the exam table, holding her head.

"Stop that," she said. "I want some anesthesia." She sucked in some air as if trying to hold back sniffles.

"Look here," I said, "I told you you can't have none. Anesthetic is nothing to monkey with. You might have a severe allergic reaction to it. No, I'm pretty sure chances are good you *will* have a severe reaction. We can't take that chance for such a wee little cut."

Francesca nodded in agreement.

Della Frasier kept glaring at me. She shook her head like a child refusing to come closer.

"Get back up here so we can finish," Francesca said. She patted the creased tissue paper covering the table. "You can go home when we're all done."

"But you said I needed fifteen stitches," Della Frasier said. "That don't sound like no wee little cut."

Now my cold spot was twisting and turning as if running down long hallways and doubling back at dead ends. I waited a good fifteen seconds or so before I said anything. I wanted to keep Della Frasier in suspense. She was making my whole office smell like macaroni & cheese.

"Well," I finally said, "maybe you can have just a taste of anesthetic."

Francesca looked at me.

"A taste?" Della Frasier said.

I patted the tissue paper too. I smiled the most reassuring smile I could. I told her maybe I was wrong, maybe she would be okay with just a little taste. It was hard to know for sure if someone would have a negative reaction, I explained, and sometimes it was better to be safe than sorry. That's why I'd said no at first. But she was a strong woman to be able to jump off the table like that with a head injury, I also explained, so maybe it would be all right to give her just a taste. And just a taste was all she needed to make it not hurt at all. Not a bit.

She cautiously lay down on the exam table again, never taking her eyes off me. "A taste?" she repeated. She had amusement in her eyes now, like she thought she'd won.

"No more than a taste," I said, "or you might could still

get a nasty reaction, maybe even an infection, and *die*." I tried to look suddenly grave before I smiled in reassurance once more.

Francesca's eyes met mine again. *Might could?* she mouthed quietly. She rolled her eyes.

"We don't want me to die," Della Frasier said.

"You let me finish this and get you on the mend, and you'll be eating your cereal at the drug store for years and years," I said. "With Violet."

I asked Francesca to hold her down tightly. She wrinkled her nose and hesitated but complied. And I explained to Della Frasier that the anesthetic was just a tad bitter and might make her flinch. If she moved even the slightest, it would slow down the effect.

"Ready?" I said.

Della Frasier jiggled her head up and down quickly.

"Okay," I said. "Where's my car battery?"

"Hmm?" she said, eyes suddenly wide, head jerking toward me.

I jabbed her right in the middle of her cut, in a spot still bleeding fresh. She yelled Ow several more times very fast. She kicked and wriggled and struggled to push Francesca off her. My knee was tickling at this point as if being rubbed by a cold stainless-steel plate. With all of my weight on my other leg, it wasn't easy keeping my balance.

"What does it take to get you to listen?" I said. And there in Della Frasier's eyes now was a flash of recognition mixed with sudden fear.

I moved quicker than before and tried to get that first suture in yet one more time.

But Della Frasier screamed and thrashed harder. Francesca let go and backed away.

"Do you want that anesthetic or not?" I said.

"All right, all right," Della Frasier said. She was breathing hard and angry. "Your battery's in my trunk."

"There," I said, satisfied finally. "That wasn't so bad now, was it?"

SPEED
LIMIT
55

YOU SEE, MAMA talked a lot about where she grew up, but she never went back again after she moved to Chicago to be with my dad. I'd driven through Lawton with Willadeene once on our way to Florida. We went a hundred miles out of our way just to see this place we'd heard about. We only drove down the main street and through some of the neighborhoods with their brick houses, and we continued on our way south without looking back. It didn't impress us much at the time.

When Dad was very close to dying, however, it seemed a natural choice for me, the right place to start living for myself, for reasons I still don't really know.

Francesca said later on that she'd never seen Della Frasier so sheepish and embarrassed. After giving the poor old woman some anesthetic for real and sewing up her head, I retrieved my battery from her trunk. She refused my prescription for narcotics. Her Fairmont nagged and stalled, nagged and stalled. Then it puffed and clanked, and she drove away with a roar. I reconnected my battery while two boys across the street were shooting off cap guns and twirling sparklers around and around. Except for the caps popping, no sound at all came from the little town under the brutal sun and the net of smokesmell riding in on the breeze from far away. I started up my car. The thirty or so miles north to Francesca's mama and stepdad's little place on Lake Chickamahonny were uneventful. The rest of the day passed slowly and easily, Francesca's lilac perfume fresh and lovely.

Around midnight, after a late dinner of poke salad, roasted corn, and dark chocolate dipped in chardonnay, Francesca and I walked down the path through the woods to the lake. The heat had lessened, the full moon was out, and a bluish-gray haze bled through the trees. The smell of smoke was much stronger than before and had been growing stronger all day. The cool spot on my knee throbbed minutely along to the rhythm of the song Francesca faintly sang while we walked.

Don't sing love songs, you'll wake my mother…

Reeds and cattails grew along the water's edge. At the dock, we untied Francesca's antique wooden rowboat and pushed off. Gleaming black letters on the bow proudly proclaimed the boat *The Tennessee Scrambler*. Francesca sat in back, facing me, and told me the story of the boat's name.

Her daddy had a houseboat moored on Isle of Palms not too far from his beach house, she said, and he used the houseboat to host parties on Saturday nights. Though he kept it moored permanently, and it certainly wasn't a fast boat by any means, he'd named this houseboat *The Tennessee Scrambler*. Francesca talked about how he invited and welcomed all the out-of-town tourists from up and down the beach, and after the sun went down they came dressed in their tropical finest—the men in linen pants and Hawaiian shirts and the women in sarongs and sandals—and bringing wine and deserts and rum and fruit. Her daddy wanted everyone at these parties to tell their best story or joke, so they all took turns, their stories getting more and more outrageous and bawdy as daylight approached and one by one the guests either stumbled back to their rented beach houses or passed out drunk. Her daddy called these parties Scramble Nights, she said, because, as he'd put it, he liked the scrambled variety of tales that would no doubt be told.

And so Francesca had named her boat *The Tennessee Scrambler* too.

I took up the creaky oars and navigated us through a group of partially submerged stumps near the dock, and I rowed us slowly down to the railroad trestle on the far side of the lake, where we anchored underneath the tracks.

We waited for the train. The moon was high above the weeping willows. Mosquitoes hung over the lake. The water's shiny surface seemed to vibrate as subtly as a tuning fork. The smoke drifting in from afar rolled around us.

Where that fire was burning, it was getting closer, I thought. Maybe too close.

A whistle blasted and wailed from about a mile away. The train soon rumbled slowly overhead, and Francesca and I watched its wheels spark in the night, felt the humid, smoky air twist around us as the cars swayed back and forth above. The last car passed about twenty minutes later, and the train clattered away, around the bend past the lake. Gone.

Francesca started the same song again.

All men are fools, so says my mother...

We stayed anchored under the railroad bridge a while. Mosquitoes buzzed and cicadas droned. A songbird burbled a melody somewhere nearby. It abruptly stopped, and wings quickly flapped and grew faint far away.

Beware, beware the silver dagger...

Suddenly the lake sparkled like a flat mirrorball, its ripples reflecting fireflies that came zipping out from the reeds and cattails and skimmed above the water and twirled in all directions around us up and over and down and back and forth and up again in rapid spirals, leaving pink, purple, blue, and green scribble trails of lingering light behind, a giant, glowing cross-stitch pattern.

The smoke had grown heavier and denser almost without us noticing it, that's how fast the fire seemed to be coming.

"Clinton, row us back to the middle of the lake," Francesca said, spears of concern in her voice, almost as if reading my mind.

I pulled up the anchor and started rowing. The smoke was wispy and stretched around us like wide, dusty spider webs. My lungs felt as if something inside them was scratching for a way out. I coughed and rubbed my eyes, and so did Francesca. She found an old dirty towel under the seat, ripped it in two, and dipped both pieces into the water. We held them dripping wet over our mouths and noses.

A loud crackling burst forth from somewhere close by, followed by a whooping siren that grew in pitch and volume as it approached. And there were the flames. They came swift and vengeful. Orange and yellow and blue and green, climbing up the trees, sweeping over the reeds and cattails.

The fireflies stayed near us in the middle of the lake

beyond the fire's reach. They flew so fast we saw only their trails spinning circles that enclosed the boat. As the temperature rose from the fire, the cold in my knee plummeted until I could no longer flex my leg. Francesca and I held each other, wet towels on our faces.

And down below us, even farther beyond the reach of the fire, a log cabin still stood. Though it was submerged, it was waiting for its owners to appear from the woods after a hunt or picnic, stamp up the stairs, cross the threshold, and settle down for the night, home. But all the windows were empty and black. The light from the fire above reflected in them like garish anemones.

A small round face calmly peeked out from one of the windows, watching and waiting. The face was that of a baby girl. Her eyes were big and blue. Her pursed little lips were a dull pink. Bubbles came out of her mouth. Her fair skin was sunburned. Her hair was curly and blond. It waved in the murky hell-lit water. She turned away from the window, stepped down off the upside-down bushel basket she was standing on to see out, and retreated deeper into the underwater cabin.

The water pressure pricked my ears. My frozen leg was a lead weight. When my lungs felt as if they were about to burst, I pulled Francesca by the hand and kicked and stroked back up toward the surface in the direction of the awful hot light, the smoke, the fireflies, the fire-warped rowboat, the trees wrenching and crying as their branches fell flaming, and the distant moon and stars over everything.

SPEED LIMIT 55

SISTER MELVINA

IT'S A SECRET. BUT YOU can take it from me. Before I continue any further, however, you must think about a few things. First, a true traveler always drives the car like he stole it. Second, never start with *Before I begin, I'd like to say a few words about myself.* Nobody cares about you. People are going to peg you from the story you tell anyway.

Now that that's out of the way, I have it on good authority that the citizens of Copperkroger still owned kites when they weren't supposed to. Of course this means they traded kites on the black market too, and even bought them outright from the secret manufacturers at wholesale prices.

Copperkroger — a city in the north. I suppose the situation is even more interesting when you realize that the people of Copperkroger were the ones who started the great kite war many years ago to end such things. You might remember that the people of Copperkroger won this very war under the leadership of their former mayor who had gone on to become president of the country after a scandalous election that rewrote the country's constitution. This was how he could declare war on cities in his own country and stay in office. After the victory of the militia from Copperkroger, the people of every other city in the country were forced to hide their kites away. Notice I didn't say they were forced to set their kites free. This was not the point.

And so the people of every other city in the country reeled in their kitestrings on bright yellow, pink, and orange spools, and their kites dipped and turned, and dipped again, and swooped in low until either sliding to a nice stop on their bellies or crashing on their noses. Hands, some leathery and cracked, some delicate and fine, pulled apart the kites, folded them together, and locked them away in attics or in basements. Legend has it some people even burned their kites.

This was all done very quickly. The people of every other city in the country did not want to face further destruction at the hands of the militia of Copperkroger and the president who had once been mayor.

Every year, however, for two undisclosed days in February, the officials of Copperkroger prohibited anyone from outside from entering the city. Air traffic was rerouted so that nobody flew overhead. Shipping came to a stop on all highways entering town, and trucks sat idle for two days until the okay was given to proceed in to their drop-off points. Sentries perched on the outlying hills with special sensors to be sure nobody was looking at the city from a distance through a telescope.

The people of Copperkroger brought out their secret kites, and everyone—and I mean each and every person who lived in the city—closed up everything and walked down to the big frozen lake in the center of town, where they flew their kites from the ice. Tents went up on the ice too, and vendors of all kinds stocked these tents with all kinds of kites imaginable. Some sold food—hot dogs, chili, cocoa, cinnamon-roasted almonds. The chocolaty, meaty, and cinnamon-nutty smells drifted over the frigid city like a protective tarp, and the wind blew over the lake and made the fresh snow dance between people's legs.

The people waddled around on the ice in bright snowsuits, moonboots, mittens, scarves, and hats. They looked like jelly rolls. One year when I was in Copperkroger at the time of the kite festival, I witnessed it all myself. Of course I had to hide under a comforter in the backseat of a rusty old Cadillac until the officials made their sweep of the town in search of outsiders, and after that I had to disguise myself as a citizen of Copperkroger. Which, as you know, is not terribly hard to do.

Getting back to my main story, at the kite festival I saw a woman in a hat that looked like the Eiffel Tower. The hat was almost as tall as she was, and she didn't take it off until a crazy kite swooped in low and snagged on it.

But the kites. Such magnificent things. And three-dimensional. One a big black cat pouncing after a yellow canary. Another a dragon breathing fire. Another an airplane much like the one the former mayor of Copperkroger who is now the president of the country flies in. Another a genie emerging from a bottle. All these kites were tied to stakes driven into the ice so that the hands of their owners wouldn't get tired. Yes, hundreds and hundreds of kites of all sizes, colors, and shapes, with streamers and tails, and bells, some even with payloads of lightbulbs that were dropped in a shattering crescendo of glass on the ice. All of these kites flew over the frozen lake like a huge banner above the city.

I'm only supposing, however, that the kites looked like a huge banner. Nobody alive, except for the sentries, has ever gotten close enough to Copperkroger during the kite festivities to witness this from another perspective, and, you see, everyone in Copperkroger was on the lake, right under all the kites. And the sentries certainly never declared (under penalty of extradition) what they thought the kites looked like, so how would anyone have known all the kites together looked like a huge banner flying over the city? To the Copperkroger citizens on the ice, all the kites probably looked like — and I must say they looked like this to me too — a huge umbrella, or how about a parachute?

As I was saying, some kites did acrobatic tricks in time to patriotic orchestra music blasting from speakers set up at various locations around the frozen lake.

But it all ended last week. Sister Melvina was my great-grandmother's sister, so that made Sister Melvina my great-great-aunt. Sister Melvina never missed the secret annual kite-flying. Her favorite part of the whole event was buying hot cocoa from the cocoa tent. But she didn't drink it. Nobody knows why — and I don't know why either because she never told me — but every year she shook her Styrofoam cup once like a priest shakes a holy water scepter, and her cocoa sprinkled all over the snow outside the tent. Sister Melvina said once that the drops of cocoa melting through the snow looked like gunshot wounds. The drops melted right through the snow and ice to the cold, dark water below. Sister Melvina poked a stick down a hole one year to see, and it came up wet.

So, when you say that someone isn't playing with a full deck, just what cards do you think they're not playing with?

People should have been concerned. But they weren't. Nobody ever paid her any attention. I always wondered how the ice could support all those people on it at one time, and, to tell you the truth, Sister Melvina was always a little afraid, in spite of what she knew she had to do. Nothing could draw her away from the power of the kites, however, so, holes through the ice or not, she mustered up her faith and went every year to splash her cocoa regardless.

She was a sight to see. Her long black robes flapped and cracked in the wind, her habit flailed behind her as if it were a kite itself, her face, even though a hundred years old, gleamed smooth and white as the undisturbed snow on the far corner of the lake where nobody flew kites. She laughed too, waved her arms up and down, and spun round and round until her little feet in little black Sister shoes slipped on the ice and she fell down in a black heap and her robes billowed around her. She pushed away people who asked if she'd broken her hip and tried to help her up. She sat by her cluster of hot cocoa spots in the snow and laughed under the February sun until dusk, when the wind died and the kites all came down.

This year in particular was the last year for Sister Melvina to cast her hot cocoa over the ice. She knew it was time. It was the last year anybody from Copperkroger flew a kite, for that matter. The routine was the same. Incoming traffic grumbled in clouds of exhaust in the bitter cold, the sky sparkled in its absence of airplane trails, and the sentries held one hand up to their earpieces and used their other hands to bring their microphones closer to their mouths.

Hammers pounded stakes into the ice, and the ice screeched every inch the stakes dug in. The kites went up—many of them were the same ones that flew the year before, and the year before that, and so on. The wind tugged at the taut strings tied to the stakes. The lady who once wore the Eiffel Tower hat now came in a plain purple stocking cap with a yellow fluffy ball on top.

Great-great-aunt Sister Melvina carefully edged her way down the boat ramp leading to the lake's frozen surface. Her robes snapped in the wind, and her shoes squeaked on the ice and the fresh snow that had fallen the night before. She held her robes tight at her throat, squinted in the noon sun, and watched the kites for a while.

She made her way past a crackling loudspeaker playing the country's national anthem, and she entered the hot cocoa tent. She gave the man in front two silver coins and a folded green bill. She picked up the steaming Styrofoam cup with her bare hands, sniffed the chocolate, and closed her eyes and sighed. She must have been a little sad, knowing this was the last year, but she wasn't afraid now.

When she went outside again—*Hello, Sister*, someone said—she raised the cup above and behind her head and flicked the hot cocoa forward. The hot cocoa sprayed all over the ice and snow in front of her. Again, nobody paid any attention to her. They'd all seen her do this year after year after year.

The hot cocoa melted through the snow—no surprise there—and bored straight through the ice. No surprise there either. But the chocolaty brown holes that looked like bullet wounds widened until the holes were as big around as telephone poles. They widened some more.

Some people stopped. The Eiffel Tower lady in her purple stocking cap gaped and pointed. A boy ran by and tripped on a kite stake because he was staring at the holes instead of watching where he was running.

And the holes kept growing. And growing.

Sister Melvina did her yearly little dance until she fell. She closed her eyes and prayed.

By this time the holes were as big around as limousines. Some holes came together and made bigger holes. A tent collapsed in the water when the ice disappeared from under it. People screamed, threw their arms up in the air, and vanished in the dark, icy lake. Their heavy snowsuits soaked with water, and they sank right to the bottom before they could put up much of a struggle. In all the panic, the Eiffel Tower lady caught her neck on a kite string and choked when the string wrapped around her. She too settled on the bottom of the lake after the ice evaporated under her feet and water filled her lungs.

Soon the entire lake had thawed. Kites, no longer staked down, drifted in the wind until they flopped to a soft landing on the buildings downtown or on the snow-covered ground far from the lake. They skipped and whirled down the empty streets of the city, snagged in empty trees, and caught their strings in television antennas.

Sister Melvina levitated a few inches over the water with

her eyes closed. Tents with air trapped under them skimmed and rolled across the lake with the wind. Kites with long streamers and tails flopped and settled all over the water like a rain of confetti.

But one kite, the black cat pouncing after a canary, rose higher and higher. Sister Melvina opened her eyes and watched it. Its line whipped past her, and she grabbed it just before it ran out. The kite raised her up, and she soared with it high above the city, up to the sky, her robes and her habit rippling and singing.

I don't know where she went, where the kite took her. But after that she was nowhere to be found in the empty city of Copperkroger. After emergency crews from the capitol of the country cleared the kites away so the television cameras wouldn't see them, the president of the country who was once the mayor of Copperkroger flew in and gave a solemn speech in front of city hall, which was empty. He considered himself lucky to be alive. Had he still been mayor of Copperkroger he also would have perished.

And Sister Melvina's convent was empty. Her church was empty. The factories were empty, and so were the stores, public restrooms, hotels, schools, movie theaters, and that rusty old Cadillac. Everything. Empty. That's how Sister Melvina thought things should be.

And how do I know all this? Like I said, a true traveler always drives the car like he stole it, nobody cares, and so on and so forth. That means that sometimes the only point is the story itself, and the teller is irrelevant. Excuse me, please, while I step out for some fresh air and an amaretto sour.

SPEED LIMIT
55

ABOUT THE AUTHOR

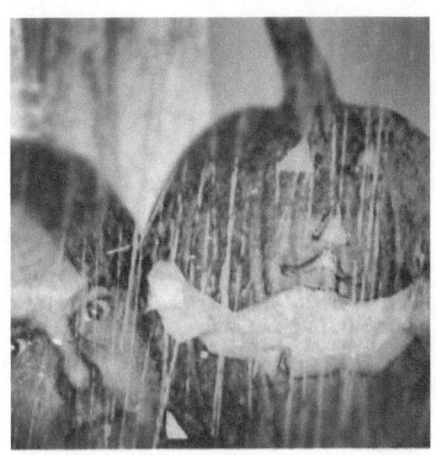

STEPHEN ROGER POWERS is the author of three poetry collections published by Salmon Poetry in Ireland. He has worked as a stand-up comic and a delivery driver. If you look closely in the right place, you can see him as an extra in *Joyful Noise* with Queen Latifah and Dolly Parton. He is now an English professor, and *Highway Speed* is his first collection of short stories.

www.stephenrogerpowers.com

www.ingramcontent.com/pod-product-compliance
Lightning Source LLC
Chambersburg PA
CBHW020637260626
47157CB00008B/2788

* 9 780578 583983 *